"Thank you for this evening." The warmth of his knee pressed against hers. Heat exploded through her, spiraling down her spine in a burst of passion that made her gasp. **"I enjoyed myself very much."**

He set his wine down on a nearby table and then took her hand. "For a moment, I thought I was going to lose you to the media." He brought her fingers to his mouth and kissed the tips.

"Not a chance." Her skin tingled. She almost snatched her hand back at the flare of desire touching him roused in her. "Have you finally decided I'm not going to hurt your father?"

"I've decided I want to kiss you." He slid his arms around her and pulled her to him. He leaned against a chair flanking the fireplace and gathered her close to him. She closed her eyes, taking in the feel of his body next to hers, his fingers on her skin.

Goose bumps rose on her arms. Her breath caught in her throat. His lips were warm and soft against her, and his breath fanned across her cheek. She breathed deeply of his scent, which was like a forest after a rain.

D1359961

Books by J. M. Jeffries

Harlequin Kimani Romance

Virgin Seductress
My Only Christmas Wish
California Christmas Dreams

J. M. JEFFRIES

is the collaboration between two women who are lifelong romance-aholics. Jacqueline Hamilton grew up believing that life should always have a happy ending. Being a military brat, she has lived in some of the most romantic places in the world. An almost lawyer, Jackie decided to chuck it all, live her dream and become a writer. Miriam Pace grew up believing in fairy tales. She found her Prince Charming and has been married to him for thirty-seven years. Now a granny, she is reading fairy tales to her grandson.

California
CHRISTMAS
DREAMS

J. M. JEFFRIES

HARLEQUIN® KIMANI™ ROMANCE

To Mark, who is fighting the good fight.

Recycling programs
for this product may
not exist in your area.

ISBN-13: 978-0-373-86329-7

CALIFORNIA CHRISTMAS DREAMS

Copyright © 2013 by Miriam A. Pace and Jacqueline S. Hamilton

HARLEQUIN®
™ www.Harlequin.com

Printed in U.S.A.

Dear Reader,

Who doesn't love roller coasters, carousels and waterslides? Theme parks have become a staple for entertainment and family fun, from the start of a theme park legacy in California to the mighty roller-coaster extravaganzas people love to fear.

I hope you enjoy Jake and Merry's story as they find a way to bring a run-down amusement park back to life while facing both emotional challenges and personal choices. From romantic rides on the carousel to walks on the beach, Jake and Merry discover finding love is the greatest roller-coaster ride of all.

Much love,

Jackie and Miriam

J. M. Jeffries

Acknowledgments

Shannon Criss, thank you for believing in J. M. Jeffries. Also, thank you to the wonderful, wonderful people at Harlequin who work so hard for romance.

Chapter 1

Meredith Alcott sat stiffly in the HR director's office, wondering what lurked behind Susan Moran's smile. Susan was impeccably dressed in a platinum-gray suit and pink blouse, and had a pin in the shape of a turtle on the lapel of her jacket. Tully the Turtle, Susan's favorite animated character, seemed to be waving at her, but Merry didn't feel like waving back.

Susan's straight hair was carefully brushed to one side and braided to hang down over her shoulder. Merry always felt a little grubby in Susan's presence. Today was no different, no matter that she'd carefully styled her curly black hair and was wearing her most stylish black silk pantsuit.

Almost every surface in Susan's office was decorated with Tully the Turtle memorabilia—from the huge turtle clock on the wall to the dainty watch on her wrist. Tully the Turtle had been Bernard and William Chapman's original animated character and had made a fortune for the two men and their family. Enough that they could build their own studios and eventually their tie-in theme park.

Like Merry, Susan had been a child actress for Chapman Brothers Studios. The brothers took care of all their employees, even the child actors who'd grown up and left acting.

"I've been with the Chapman Brothers since I was a child, Susan," Merry said patiently. "This is the second opening in the studio's design department I've applied for in the past five years, and the second time I've been turned down. I would like to know why." Merry gave a polite smile even as she dreaded the answer. In the back of her mind, she always wondered if she wasn't good enough. *Nonsense,* she told herself sternly. She was good enough, but the nagging little doubt remained.

Susan straightened the pens lined up on the side of her desk. Everything about Susan was neat and tidy despite the clutter of her office. "Your credentials are impeccable and we appreciate your loyalty, but Lisa Chapman just graduated from college." Susan paused, letting the information hang in the air. Then she sighed. "I take orders, too, and I'm so sorry you're unhappy." A look of regret passed over her face. She reached for a business card and a pencil, and started to write.

Merry nodded politely, swallowing her disappointment. She wanted to throw a good old-fashioned hissy fit: roll on the ground and scream and cry. Then she'd get fired, go broke and lose her house. She, her shoes and her cat would be homeless. That was a bit of an exaggeration; she did have money set aside. Thank goodness for residuals. But not even the residuals were enough to pay her mortgage and keep her in organic food. "Thank you, Susan, for talking to me."

"I know you're disappointed," Susan said, adding something else to the business card in front of her. "This is the contact information for John Walters. He owns the Citrus Grove Entertainment Center in Riverside. I'll be honest with you. Management is going to keep you dangling for another five years. And there's no guarantee that the next opening that comes available will go to you. Maybe it's time you made a change. Call this man and talk to him."

Merry accepted the card, hiding her surprise. She put it in her pocket, stood up and smiled as cordially as she could. "I appreciate that," she said. Then she turned and left the large, airy office.

In the parking garage, Merry leaned against her brand-new Prius hybrid car, trying not to cry. August heat swirled around her, making her silk blouse stick to her back. Lisa Chapman was family, and Merry understood that. But what about Merry? The Chapman brothers prized loyalty, and she'd been loyal. Giving the job she'd worked for to Lisa hurt. Did fresh-out-of-college Lisa Chapman know more about designing sets than Merry did?

When she'd heard that Eric Sloan was retiring, she'd bought a new car because she knew she was next in line to head the set-design department. She would get away from working in the theme park and move back into the TV-and-movie division, which would give her more opportunities.

She stroked the sexy, white, gas-efficient Prius for a moment, eyes closed, refusing to give in to her disappointment. The Chapman brothers knew how fleeting fame could be. As each child actor had grown up and out of the roles they played, they'd been given a place behind the scenes. Those who'd leveraged their abilities into full-blown acting careers had eventually left to continue their lives. Merry had stayed, and now she wondered why. The Chapmans had rewarded her loyalty by giving away the job she coveted to one of their own family, even though Lisa's degree was so new the ink wasn't dry. She'd interned at the park under Merry and had mentioned she'd wanted the job. Sure, she'd work for a salary half of what Merry would command, but that didn't make it fair. Merry had been faithful to the Chapman brothers, but they hadn't reciprocated.

She opened her car door and slid into the stuffy interior. She started the motor and waited for the air conditioner to spit out cold air before she put the thing in gear and headed back to Redlands. As much as she loved working for the Chapman Brothers theme park, she had the feeling she would never get out of it. She wanted more than just being told what to do and occasionally adding suggestions for the design of the rides, the seasonal display changes and the floral arrangements surrounding the ticket booths. She wanted more creative input. She didn't want to be a gofer forever.

Just before she threw the car in gear, her phone rang. "Hi, Noelle."

"Are we drinking, or are we shoe shopping?" her sister asked.

"We're drinking," Merry answered. Shoe shopping was the victory dance.

"Monkey nuts!" Noelle said. "What happened?"

"They gave the job to a relative who just graduated from University of California, Riverside." Saying the words out loud upset her all over again. Merry had started working for the studio two days after her seventh birthday, appearing as an extra on a number of series before landing the role of Maddie Jefferson's best friend. She'd loved working on *Maddie's Mad World,* but she'd wanted to be the star of her own show. And now she was still stuck being second banana, which was why she'd left acting at eighteen to attend UCLA's design school. She was a talented set designer, and she wanted to put those talents to use. Some people worked for a mouse, some for a duck and she worked for a turtle that seemed to move backward more often than forward.

"What are you going to do?" Noelle asked.

"I'm going to come over to your house after work, think about my options and drink all of your tequila." She fingered the card Susan had given her. It had one name on it, John Walters, and his phone number. She'd heard about Citrus Grove Park. She'd even gone once to check it out, but hadn't been impressed. The park was aging and showing its unadorned bones. It needed a face-lift and a Botox injection.

"I'll make guacamole and put clean sheets on the spare bed," Noelle said.

"I should be there around eight-thirty," Merry replied and disconnected.

She put the Prius in gear and pulled out of the garage onto hot Burbank Street.

Jacob Walters sat in his office overlooking Hollywood Boulevard. Nineteen-year-old Annie Gray sat in front of him, her legs curled up under her, a kittenish, wide-eyed smile on her elfin face. She had a fey, waiflike look, as well as an atrocious sense of style. Today she wore pink shorts, a yellow shirt with some sort of odd design on it and purple lipstick. Her brown hair, pulled into an untidy braid, was streaked with dark pink and orange.

Thick black liner around her blue eyes made her look like a raccoon.

"So tell me," he said, "what exactly do you do with a ten-thousand-dollar belt?"

Annie pouted. "It's Hermès. It's a status symbol."

Annie Gray was an up-and-coming recording artist with the voice of an angel, the beauty of a swan and the mouth of a truck driver. Annie's mother had hired Jake to help her manage Annie's money, but the singer was not being particularly cooperative.

"A symbol of what?" Jake asked, trying not to wince. As a financial advisor, he'd seen musicians come and go. Some came in poor and left poor, some came in poor and left rich. Annie wasn't going to leave rich if she kept spending the way she was.

"It says I'm a star." She batted her eyes at him.

He wanted to tell her she was stupid to think she would always be a star. "I know having money to spend on anything you want has its allure, but you have to think about the future."

Annie shrugged. "I have enough money. I don't need to worry."

"You will if you keep buying ten-thousand-dollar belts."

Again she shrugged. "I can't do drugs no more, so I shop."

Jake closed his eyes and prayed for patience. He would just have to ignore that issue. "Until you get back to work, you have to stick to your budget. On my advice, your mother canceled all your credit cards. You will be on a limited allowance until you're working again."

"You can't do that. It's my money." She jumped to her feet, looking panicked.

"You just got out of rehab. Nobody cares who you

were. And right now you're a sort-of-famous, ex-junkie pop star whose only claim to fame is a song about sexting. I'm doing what I can to keep you solvent."

She sauntered over to the edge of his desk, unbuttoning the top two buttons of her shirt and pulling the edges apart to show more skin and an evil-looking tattoo that curled around the inside of her breast. She leaned over and smiled at him. "Come on, Jakie. My mummy will listen to you. Tell her I'll be a good girl. Let me keep at least one credit card."

Jake sighed. Phase two. If pouting didn't work, try seduction. She ran her fingers up his arm and he pulled away. He was thirty-two years old and had seen just about everything in the ten years he'd worked as a financial advisor. He pressed a button under his desk and a moment later his assistant, Vicki, silently opened the door and entered. "Just so you know, my secretary is standing right behind you as a witness to this meeting."

Annie jumped back and rebuttoned her blouse. "This isn't over."

Phase three: the threat. "You don't seem to understand what a conservatorship means. You have no control over your money because you can't be trusted. That is no one else's fault but yours."

"You're fired," she snapped.

"And you can't fire me, either," he said with a half smile as she moved to phase four. Like so many others before her, she was completely predictable. "I've seen it all, sweetie. Your mother has your best interests at heart and you need to grow up and listen to her."

"If I'd listened to my mother, I would have gone to college and not been a star," she snapped.

"If you'd gone to college, you could have taken an accounting class and learned to manage your own money."

"You're mean," Annie said, the pout returning. "How do I know you're not trying to rip me off and take a piece of the pie for yourself?"

Phase five, he thought, was questioning his ability to keep her solvent. "Probably because I have a lot more money than you do and don't need your piddly little 1.6 million." Which she wouldn't have if he hadn't been hired by her family.

"You're just an accountant. You can't have more money than me." She lifted her chin defiantly as though he'd be intimidated.

He resisted the urge to laugh. "I don't buy ten-thousand-dollar belts." Or fancy cars, or designer clothes. He'd bought his last Mercedes SUV used and lived in a small house in the Hills that he'd bought in a foreclosure sale. The only areas he'd splurged on had been his bedroom and the kitchen. Jake liked to cook and he wanted the best appliances he could afford. He also liked to sleep comfortably, so he did purchase a custom-made Swiss mattress that was so comfortable he fell asleep almost the moment his head touched the pillow.

She stomped her foot. "I'm going to go see a lawyer."

Phase six: the final threat—seeing a lawyer. "Fine," he replied. "See you later."

She marched out of the office, slamming the door so hard the photos on the walls bounced.

"She's going to be trouble," Vicki said.

"Like we haven't had that before," he said with a sigh. Most of his clients were trouble with a capital *T*. And Miss Gray was proving to be one of the bigger ones.

"This is a heck of a way to make a living," Vicki said, straightening one of the photos that had slipped askew from Annie's door slam.

"That's why I love it." And he did, despite the juvenile behavior of so many of his clients. He loved the challenge of putting them back on solid ground. Many of them appreciated his efforts, but a few, like Annie, chafed under his control.

"Your sister called," Vicki said. "I said you'd get back to her."

He picked up the phone as Vicki walked out, closing the door quietly behind her.

He dialed his sister. Evelyn answered on the first ring as though she'd been standing right next to the phone.

"It's Daddy. He's lost his mind."

Jake's first thought was that his widowed father had run off with a twenty-year-old bimbo. Not that his father was easily led, but a pretty woman was a pretty woman, and he'd been a widower for a long time. "What's going on?"

"He's decided he's not selling the park and is going to renovate instead. He's already been to the bank and gotten a loan."

Jake pinched the bridge of his nose. He and his father had talked about this. John Walters had inherited his family's orange groves and had proceeded to turn them into an amusement park. With the downturn in the economy, the park had been suffering until Jake had finally convinced his father to sell to developers who'd been trying to get their hands on the property for nearly ten years.

"Did you hear me, Jake?" Evelyn asked, her voice sharp.

"I'm trying to pretend this is just a bad dream, but I heard you."

"He's turning his nose up at thirty million dollars," Evelyn huffed. "And he's planning some huge Christmas extravaganza to reopen the park with and has hired some woman, a has-been child actress to do the decorations at an obscene salary. She's going to bankrupt him. Probably trying to bankroll her comeback."

"That's Dad's decision," Jake said calmly, though he agreed with his sister. Thirty million dollars was a lot of money to turn down to keep an aging amusement park open.

"I beg your pardon?" Evelyn asked, almost angrily.

"He doesn't need the money," Jake said. Jake's father had been his first client. Originally his mother had handled the finances, but when she'd passed away, Jake had taken over even though he had only been sixteen. Jake had found he was good at handling money, and by the time he'd graduated high school he'd known exactly what he was going to do for a living.

"That's not the point," Evelyn replied. "He's sixty-seven years old and should be sailing off into the sunset with one of his, you know, one of his honeys. He should be enjoying life instead of being at the park from six in the morning until midnight. He works too hard. He should be enjoying his retirement."

"So you think Dad should sail off into the sunset with some gold digger?" The image amused Jake. While his father enjoyed the charms of the opposite sex, he wasn't about to ask one on a cruise or be swayed to give her money.

"As if you'd let anyone touch his money," Evelyn scoffed.

Jake said nothing as his thoughts raced. His father was of sound mind and body. And even though Jake had argued for the sale, he'd seen that his father was torn. On one hand, the amusement park was a family legacy, but on the other hand, it was a lot to take care of.

"What are you going to do?" Evelyn asked.

"Nothing." He was disappointed in his father's decision but not terribly surprised. His father was having a hard time letting go of his family's heritage. Family meant a lot to John Walters.

"But…"

"Sis," Jake interrupted, "the property belongs to him, and he's of sound mind."

"We all agreed he would sell. He sat at the dinner table with us and listened to our arguments and agreed with everything we said. My God, if he's going to keep that damn park, my son is going to want to work there again. He's already talking about skipping college and working for his grandpa, ruining his entire future."

"He'll change his mind." He loved his sister. Evelyn had worked hard to get her doctorate in physics. She now taught at Cal State, San Bernardino and was on track to head the department.

Evelyn ground her teeth in frustration. "Can't we go to court and stop him somehow?"

"Do you really want to try to have our father declared incompetent?"

A strangled sob came to him through the phone. "No, I guess not. It's not your kids he's filling with ideas that life is an amusement park and a little orange marmalade on sourdough toast will solve everything."

Jake half smiled. His father had tried to sell him and Evelyn the same dream, but they hadn't been converted.

"I'll talk to him," Jake promised, and ended the call.

He leaned back in his chair and looked out the window at the cloudless, blue Los Angeles sky. In the distance he could see the huge Hollywood Hills sign. One of the reasons he'd taken this spot was because he loved looking at the sign.

Evelyn was right; the man had lost his mind. Jake had spent six months putting the sale together, and his father was supposed to take the money and relax for the rest of his life. What had happened? He reached for the phone, intending to call his father, but then decided maybe a trip to Riverside would be better.

Chapter 2

Merry stood in the center of her new office looking around. The room was a bit dingy, with gray paint on the walls, limp blinds on the windows and a battered desk, but she'd fix that with a little paint. A worktable was pushed against one wall, angled to catch the light from the window. The desk was a little battered, but Merry was a master at making old things look new again. Her whole house was a testament to her ability to take anything and make it look fresh and inviting.

She opened a box and started rummaging through it. Christmas lights spilled out. She found her electronic Santa Claus and hugged it. Her father had given it to her for her birthday. One of the things she'd hated as a child had been the fact she'd been born on Christmas, but her mother had solved the dilemma and celebrated her birthday on July 25. But that didn't stop her father from giving her Christmas-themed gifts. As an airline pilot, he traveled the world and often brought back unique items for Merry and her sister.

A knock sounded on the door.

"Come in," she called.

The door opened and John Walters walked in. He was a tall, broad-shouldered man with a round face, close-cropped gray hair already turning white and twinkling brown eyes. "Are you decorating for Christmas already? It's August."

"Getting in the mood," she answered. She placed the Santa on the corner of her desk and plugged it in. "And looking for inspiration. I don't have a lot of time to plan the Christmas decorations and get them up for your grand reopening." John wanted to open the day after Thanksgiving and she had a lot of work to do. She pressed the button on the Santa and "Jingle Bell Rock" blared out at her. She grinned, suddenly feeling happier than she had since she'd made her decision to leave the safety of the Chapman Brothers theme park.

She'd always have a job with them, but accepting John's offer gave her a new opportunity to shine. She didn't want to play second banana anymore. She wanted more.

The song ended and John grinned at her. He looked into the box and pulled out another package of Christmas lights. "This is a good start."

"Since you're here, would you like to see my preliminary sketches?" She walked over to her worktable and turned on the light. She'd spent the past week measuring the park, the footprints of the different rides, the pathways between them and the orange trees that dotted the park. From that she'd worked up a blueprint that gave her an aerial view, though she was going to need more detail. She flipped open her notebook. "I've done four themes for you," she said. "Christmas in California is the first one."

John nodded as he glanced at the large drawing. She'd drawn a schematic diagram of the park, highlighting each section. John's original concept for his park had been to showcase the variety of activities Southern California had to offer. The Los Angeles area had its own unique activities. A person could spend the morning at the beach, then the afternoon skiing in the mountains or looking at the stars on the Hollywood Walk of Fame. John had tried to integrate those ideas into his park. Merry had to figure out how to layer a Christmas theme over the different sections and keep it cohesive with the original concept. She'd worked out four different ideas she thought could work. "I like this," John said, pointing at her first idea of implementing the glitz and glamour of Hollywood. She'd decorated the orange trees with lights and added some gift boxes with large bows to the base of a tree. She'd sketched in various L.A. landmarks, such as the Hollywood sign, in various places near the different rides.

"This is a Currier and Ives Christmas," she said, turning the page to show him the next one.

He glanced at the sleigh pulled by reindeer and nodded slightly. Another scene showed singers dressed in nineteenth-century garb. The third scene was a fireplace with stockings hanging from it and the fourth was a cute display of a Christmas tree lit up and decorated with bows.

"I'm not sure about this one," John said.

She showed him the third idea, Christmas Around the World, and he disliked it immediately. The fourth theme, Hollywood Christmas, was a series of scenes from different Christmas movies.

"That's a strong possibility," John said, but he turned

back to the first one. "I think this is the one to go with. I love the Hollywood Christmas, but Christmas in California is more accessible to children."

"Okay, then," she said with a smile. Christmas in California was her favorite, too. She wondered if she could convince her mother or her sister to make a stained glass Christmas tree for the entrance.

"I'm glad you're here," John said.

"Me, too," Merry said. She folded the rejected drawings and started making mental lists in her head. "I think my budget will just cover all of this." If she were really, really careful. Luckily her mother had taught her to pinch a penny until it turned into a quarter.

"Good. Get going."

After John left, she found herself wandering out into the park, seeing it in her mind's eye and planning the different areas. With the park empty, she could visualize the different sections and what they would look like. The Chapman Brothers theme park was never empty. Visitors thronged the park during the day, and the cleanup and maintenance crews worked at night.

Jake stood off to the side in the shade of an orange tree, watching the former child actress as she walked around the park. She wore jeans, a white T-shirt and sneakers. Curly black hair hung down to her shoulders. Her skin was the color of caramel cream, and she looked very intense as she held a notebook in her hand. Every few feet she'd stop and write something in the notebook. Then she'd turn her head first one way then another as she studied what she was looking at. Then she'd write in her notebook again and move forward a few more feet.

She was cute in a waiflike manner with slightly tilted dark eyes and smiling mouth. He remembered her from

Maddie's Mad World. He'd loved the show when he was a kid and had had a bit of a crush on Maddie's best friend, Chloe, as played by Meredith Alcott. And seeing Chloe in the flesh made his fingers tingle while a little shiver walked up and down his spine.

His phone rang. He pulled it out of his pocket and glanced at the display. He had to answer this one.

"Jake Walters," he said, and braced himself.

"You said your father was ready to sell," Harry Constantine said angrily. "What's going on, Walters? Did he have a better offer that I don't know about?"

Actually, Jake had had a number of offers once the word had gotten out his dad was thinking of selling, but he wasn't about to tell Constantine that. "I'm sorry, Mr. Constantine, but he just doesn't want to part with the park yet."

"My partners and I are deeply annoyed at this interruption to the deal."

"There hasn't been a deal yet. The property belongs to my father, sir," Jake said stiffly, wondering why Constantine thought he was going to be the one. "He doesn't have to sell if that is his decision."

"I wasted months of my time putting this offer together and getting investors. And now he decides he doesn't want to sell! That property is ready to be developed. There are five new housing projects in development in that area. Does he want more money? I'll toss another million on the pile."

"Money isn't the issue, sir." Jake wanted to be polite to this man, but his normal level of diplomacy was quickly becoming strained.

"I've wanted to purchase this property for ten years," Harry said, his voice rising.

"Sir, I apologize for my father, but he changed his

mind and that is his prerogative. Since no papers have been signed, he can do that."

"I'm talking to my lawyers." Constantine disconnected and Jake found himself listening to dead air.

That didn't go well, he thought. He wondered who would be calling next. Probably Alicia Mortensen at Kessler Investments. She and her investors had made an offer, as well. Alicia was a predator and a longtime rival of Constantine. Jake didn't want to think about all the people his father had probably antagonized because of his decision. So he went back to watching the actress. She was so engrossed in what she was doing that he doubted she'd even noticed him.

He finally found himself walking up to her. She looked up at his approach and his head did a little lurch inside his chest. She'd been pretty as a teenager, but she was beautiful now. Beautiful in a way that took his breath away. She was petite, maybe an inch or two over five feet, and had a trim, slender figure with curves in all the right places. Her face was long and a bit narrow, framed by shoulder-length black hair with a hint of curl. Her mouth was bold and pouty, and her brown eyes were intense with a fire that took his breath away.

He wondered what kind of a person she was. In his mind, actors had such fragile egos. He figured he could intimidate the hell out of her and she'd back off. Maybe even quit, and then Jake could talk to his father again. Before he had a chance to say anything, his phone rang again. He glanced at the display. "Ah, Alicia Mortensen." He sent the call to voice mail. He would deal with her later.

He walked right up to the actress, and before he could open his mouth, she smiled at him and he found himself speechless, caught up in her hypnotizing beauty. He felt like a gulping fish.

"Hi." A light breeze fluttered the tips of her curly black hair. Up close, her brown eyes had the tiniest bit of green in them.

"You must be Chloe." That was original.

Her eyebrows went up in surprise. "I think you have me confused with the name of the character I played on *Maddie's Mad World*." Her voice was sultry and low. "My name is Merry. Meredith Alcott."

"I know," Jake replied, chagrined at his mistake. "I've always wondered what child actors did after they retired."

"Some of us get jobs, some of us go into rehab, some of us just drop out of sight," she replied sweetly.

"I'm glad you're not in rehab." That sounded pretty foolish. He couldn't come up with something better?

"Me, too," she said.

"How are you planning to separate my old man from his money?"

Her eyebrows rose and she chuckled. "You must be Jake. Your sister was a bit more subtle than you." She studied him for a second and then stuck out her hand. "Nice to meet you, too."

Was that sarcasm? He opened his mouth to say something. Again, nothing came out. Apparently she wasn't threatened by him, or by his sister, and Evelyn was a bulldozer. So much for her being a frail, fragile actress. She watched him, her jaw set in determination and a look in her eyes that told him there was nothing frail or fragile about her. He looked down at her hand and saw ink smudged on two fingers. She had beautiful hands, with long, slender fingers and nails buffed to shine. He took her hand and shook it, surprised at the firmness of her grip and the softness of her skin. For a moment, wild thoughts chased themselves through his mind until he pushed them away.

"Um," he said. "Likewise." She wasn't going to rabbit on him, so what was step number two? He should have planned this better.

"Now if you'll excuse me, I have to go and spend your dad's money." She turned on her heel and walked away, her head held high.

Jake stared after her. What the hell had just happened? That petite woman had just put him in his place.

His phone rang and he retrieved it from the holder on his belt. He glanced at the caller ID. Mel Vaughn, one of his particularly difficult clients.

He answered the call. "Mel." Jake closed his eyes and pinched the bridge of his nose. "What's wrong?"

"I'm buying my child's mother a car," Mel launched into his pitch. "I found this hot Ferrari that would be perfect for me—I mean her."

"And where would *she* put a kid's car seat?" Jake asked. He'd signed off on a SUV.

"Hey, man, the Ferrari is perfect."

"I said you could buy a minivan or an SUV."

"Minivans aren't sexy," Mel whined.

And being in debt to your hairline is? "I signed off on thirty thousand for a car. You have to stick with your budget."

"I can't think about a budget," Mel whined again. "Have a heart."

Mel Vaughn was twenty-six years old, but he was acting like a child. When he'd hit bankruptcy, the court had appointed Jake to unravel his finances. Now Mel wanted a Ferrari when he still owed the IRS a chunk of change.

Jake leaned against a fence as he watched Merry measure the diameter of a small children's ride. Every time she bent over to measure something, his pulse leaped into overdrive.

"Mel," Jake said patiently. "You can't buy a Ferrari until after you pay the IRS your back taxes. If you buy a Ferrari after the deal I brokered for you with the IRS, they'll come after you."

"How are they going to find out?"

The first thing Mel would do was tweet his purchase, post a picture on his Instagram account and announce it on his Facebook page. "Do you think a high-profile case like yours isn't going to be scrutinized? People care about what you do, Mel. And trust me, the IRS monitors everything. The purchase of a Ferrari will not stay a secret for long."

"How am I going to explain it to her?" Mel asked, his whining going up a notch.

"Have her call me. I'll be the bad guy."

"But she's got her heart set on this Ferrari."

"Then she can pay for it. Thirty grand is all you're getting. Because thirty grand is all you have to spare. You're barely swimming above water, Mel." Mel was starting his career all over again. "No Ferrari," Jake said flatly. "Don't ask me again." He disconnected, not wanting to hear Mel continue to beg.

When Jake had decided on finance for his career, he'd thought dealing with celebrities would be glamorous and fun. But the reality was much harsher. He loved his job, and he loved the challenge of fixing people's broken finances, but he didn't always like the people.

His gaze landed on Merry again. She'd moved on to another ride and stood in front of it with her sketchbook cradled in one arm while her pencil moved up and down. Jake studied her, wondering what her finances looked like. She must have socked away some money, since her series had run for five years until both she and her costar had grown out of their parts. She'd done a few movies afterward, but nothing in the past decade. She drove a Prius. In a background check, he'd found out she'd been transitioned to working in the Chapman Brothers theme park as an assistant set designer, since that seemed to be something she'd enjoyed, but most of her background was a big question.

She knelt down in front of an orange tree. She measured the base and made a note in her sketchbook. Even though she was dressed in a practical manner, he could see that her jeans were well made, and though not high-end designer jeans, they weren't something she'd picked up at a discount department store.

"Jacob," his father said. "I didn't know you were here."

Caught by surprise, Jake forced his attention away from the distracting woman to his father. "Got here a few minutes ago."

His father gave him a shrewd glance. "Pretty, isn't she?"

Jake pulled his gaze away from Merry to look at his dad. "I thought we had agreed to sell the park."

His dad's gaze darkened. "I changed my mind," he said defiantly. "I don't want to sell."

"Dad, I know you didn't care much for Harry Constantine. He can be a bit of a hard-ass, but his offer is a good one. If you don't like his offer, Alicia Mortensen at Kessler Investments is interested. I've had a number of other queries about this property."

"I don't want to sell," John said, a mulish look on his face.

"This park hasn't done more then break even in years. People who come to Los Angeles go to Chapman Brothers, Knotts Berry Farm, Universal Studios or Disneyland. They don't come to Riverside."

"I'm not looking to attract the international traveler. A lot of local people can't afford a hundred bucks to get into a big, fancy park. For a family of four, that's four hundred dollars. That was my house payment when your mom and I first got married, and that was high-end. Locals can come here for thirty per person, have a great time and go home feeling like they haven't dropped a bundle. I'm not looking for the international traveler, but the local people who don't want to compete with the whole world for a day of fun."

"I think you're making a mistake, Dad," Jake said wearily, yet still determined to make one last pitch. "You can't compete with the big people, and I don't care how cheap you make it."

"I never wanted to be a big-ticket park." His father shook his head. "Do you think people don't remember Citrus Grove? Half the people who work here were attendees before they ever got a job here. And a lot of people come because their parents came here. We are about family memories. We're a vital part of this city. I never expected you or your sister to take over the park. It was never your thing, but John II loves it here. He's the future. He's why I changed my mind about selling."

"But Dad," Jake said in the soothing tone he used on his more agitated clients, "you're sixty-seven." *I'm not giving up,* Jake thought, *just making a strategic retreat.* Though he had to admire the passion in his father.

His father's gaze rested on Merry. "Sixty-seven is the new forty," his father retorted. "I don't want to retire, Jacob. I want to get up every morning and find new ways to make people happy."

In his pocket his phone vibrated, but he ignored it. It

was probably Alicia Mortensen; she didn't like being ignored. "Don't you want to sit back and have some fun?"

"I am having fun. I'm having fun with my grandkids. I'm having fun with my customers. I'm even having fun with Miss Alcott. You see her over there," John continued with a broad smile. "She's having fun, too."

Jake followed his father's gaze. "She's measuring a tree."

"Even the tree knows how to have fun, unlike you."

"I know how to have fun." He tried to think of the last time he'd actually had fun that didn't include a neurotic client. He came up blank.

"Really," John said, with a piercing look at his son.

Merry glanced up and waved at John. John waved back, his face alight with happiness. For a moment, Jake was transported back to his childhood, going round and round on the carousel. He'd been happy at that moment, but even then he'd known the park wasn't his destiny. He'd always wondered why the magic of the park had never worked for him or for Evelyn.

"Miss Alcott is a retired child actress," Jake said.

"If I remember correctly, you never missed that show she was in," his father said with a grin.

Jake stirred uncomfortably. Sometimes his father remembered the oddest things. "And you could be sailing off into the sunset in that boat you've never used."

"Not yet. I have plenty of time to sail my boat." John's gaze rested on Merry as she held her sketchbook, her hand moving rapidly.

"Maybe it's those dark circles you have under your eyes, old man," Jake said. "You look tired."

"I'm not sleeping because I'm excited about the prospect of revitalizing this park. You should take a look at her drawings. She has a vision for what the park is eventually going to look like," John said. "And I'm not just talking about Christmas."

Jake said nothing. Merry had moved over to the go-kart track, and stood beneath the shade of a palm tree. She'd retrieved a camera from her pocket and was taking a photo of the track. Then she returned to her sketchbook.

He wasn't winning this battle, but he could still win the war. Maybe what he needed to do was play along for the moment. With the new improvements, the price could go up. He could still win this. He just needed to keep his hand in everything. "You're right, Dad," Jake conceded. "Let me help you. I'll oversee the money. Keep everything on budget."

"I've been handling my own money since you left for school."

"Handling money can be a burden. Let me take that burden off your shoulders so you can concentrate on the park and have more fun with Evelyn and your grandchildren."

John glanced at his son, indecision on his face. "I never made you work in the park when you were a kid because you just didn't have it in you. But I'm going to accept your offer with gratefulness and gracefulness. Because it will make you feel better if you can keep an eye on me. If you want to pretend I'm a drooling, addlepated old man, that's okay with me." He turned around and left, whistling as he sauntered down the path toward the carousel.

Jake watched his father leave, knowing he hadn't fooled the old man, but he did feel better. This way he could keep Merry from frittering the money away on stupid stuff.

* * *

Merry sketched out an idea for the center island of
the go-kart track. In her mind's eye, she could see a
huge Christmas tree, bright with lights and large ornaments. Stacks of large boxes wrapped in different colors
with bows decorating the tops could be strewn beneath
the branches. Maybe a big fluffy dog hidden behind the
boxes would add interest.

She moved along the edge of the go-kart track, ever
conscious of Jake Walters's gaze on her. He'd be really
hot if he wasn't such a stick-in-the-mud. If only he would
smile. He had a nice face and handsome eyes, but the
austere expression and the rigid way he stood made him
seem distant and aloof. She took out her tape measure
and measured a section of fence surrounding the track.
She entered the dimensions and then counted all the
sections. She doubted she'd string any Christmas lights
around the bars, but it never hurt to have a complete picture of what she could do.

She glanced at Jake Walters standing by the flagpole,
watching her. His head was tilted to one side as he listened to his father. Despite John's enthusiasm, she could
see that Jake didn't share it. His body was stiff and un-
yielding and he clearly didn't want to listen to his father.
John's body was loose and flexible as he gestured with
his hands. She could see enthusiasm in every mannerism
John exhibited. She didn't understand why Jake didn't
get it. This park was magical in its own way. Not like the
others, but in a more down-to-earth manner.

John walked away whistling, leaving Jake standing
by the flagpole. Merry knew Jake wanted his father to
sell the park, and he would probably do what he could to
talk John into accepting the terms of the sale. Just from
the way they stood, she could tell they were both deter-

mined men. Maybe accepting this job wasn't the smartest move on her part; she'd better start thinking about contingency plans. She still had contacts at Universal Studios from her intern days, and they'd start shooting the midseason replacement shows soon. She'd worked for them for a year before the Chapman Brothers had come back to her with a better offer, but now that she'd ended that association she'd better start thinking ahead again.

"My father says you've done some drawings to show your plans for the park. May I see them?" Jake asked.

Merry started. He'd crept up on her while she'd been caught in her thoughts. "Yeah, sure," she said. "Come on." She led the way back to her dingy little office.

She spread the plans out across her desk and drawing table. She rubbed her thumb nervously against her thigh. He hadn't said a word; he simply stared at them, thumbing through the drawings.

She was deeply conscious of how he made her office seem smaller and even more dingy. He was a man who overpowered a room.

He didn't say anything for the longest time, simply glanced back and forth, his mouth pressed tightly shut. She wanted him to be impressed with her vision, but he seemed to become more and more distant.

"This is going to cost a lot of money," Jake said after a long, uncomfortable silence.

"Yes, the initial outlay is going to cost. We have sets to build and costumes to make, but what I'm planning here is something that will be multifunctional. I'll repurpose the same props for Easter, summertime, Halloween and then Christmas again. And your father gave me a budget. I think I can meet it and maybe spend even less if I can get a lot of local college students to help me with things. They get course credit and I get cheap labor."

He didn't say anything, and Merry waited uncomfortably. He looked skeptical. She racked her brain trying to think of the right things to say that would sway him. "I haven't got a hope in hell in convincing you this is a good idea. Why did you even bother to talk to me?"

Surprise lit his eyes at her directness. "Dad is sixty-seven years old. He should be tuna fishing in Cancun or chasing nubile Tahitian girls."

Her eyes opened wide. "Wow. Do you really think your dad wants to chase Tahitian girls? So we know how you intend to spend your retirement."

"Hell, no, not me," Jake said, shaking his head vigorously.

"Your dad has a lot of life left in him. Why shouldn't he do what he wants to do?"

"Because this is a dying park."

"No," she said, "not dying, just a little lost. This park doesn't know what it wants to be when it grows up."

"And you do."

She looked him directly in the eye. "Yes, I do." She took his hand and tugged him toward the door. "Come on. I want to really show you my vision."

She opened the door and dragged him out back into the park. "This park has so much potential. Nowadays, it's not enough to just look pretty. You have to provide substance, too."

"You can't remake this park into a mini Chapman Brothers."

He didn't resist the pull of her hand, but she sensed he didn't really want to come with her. Not that he dragged his feet like a child, but she felt that he had no enthusiasm for his father's dream.

"No one can compete with the Chapman Brothers. They have a studio, their own amusement park to advertise their movies and a ton of visitors who come every year from all over the world. I, of all people, would know."

"Then what's the point?" he asked as she drew him toward the miniature golf course.

"There's room for everyone. This is going to be a different experience." She drew him to a small bridge that gave him an overview of the three courses that were woven together. "Look at this. What do you see?"

"Miniature golf."

She shook her head. "Look at each course. What is the theme of each course?"

"I don't see one."

"Right. So think of each section as a microcosm of California. Hollywood on course one with famous movie posters and a miniature Hollywood sign. Maybe some lights, a few director's chairs and fake cameras. The second course could be based on the different missions in California. The basic structures are already there. We just need to tweak it a little bit. And for course three, San Francisco at its finest. The Golden Gate Bridge, Alcatraz, streetcars, Lombard Street. Each course would have its own unique theme."

His face was blank. "If you don't want to be better than competing parks, why bother?"

"I want to be different." She wanted to stamp her foot at his ignorance. "You need to see the differences. The differences are what make this place unique, and I'm going to bring all those hidden bones to the surface and make this park shine."

"And suck my father's life savings away."

"That was cruel," she said. "You don't even know me. I want to be part of this. I want to bring this park back to life. And so does your dad. It has good bones, Mr. Walters, and I think you're selling your father short. And I know you're selling me short." She turned on her heel and walked away.

Chapter 3

"I need more funds in the project's budget in order to pay the costume designer." Merry stood in what used to be John's office and was now somehow Jake's. She wasn't certain how that had happened, but instead of going to John for the money, she was arguing with Jake instead.

"This is a lot of money for just a bunch of sketches," Jake said.

Merry closed her eyes in an effort to stifle her frustration. "Candace Frenche has designed for Martin Scorsese, Joss Whedon and J.J. Abrams. She's won two Oscars in costume design. She put James Cameron on hold to do this for me—and she deeply discounted her price."

"I get that this woman is the Bentley of designers, and I don't want my dad to fail in this, but this is a lot of money for just the designs. And it's running over the costume budget."

Oh, please, please, please, Merry thought. *Don't let*

him see how horrified I am. "Did you think Candace was going to design the costumes for free?"

"I expected you to work within the budget we agreed on," Jake said. He sat behind the desk, looking calm and unruffled.

"I hire the best people I can get for a reasonable price. A lot of these people are working for me way cheaper than they do for anyone else, as a favor. I am getting you a huge deal. You can call anybody up and ask them how much they pay for Candace's services and they'll tell you. I know how to save money, but right here—" she pounded a finger on the bill "—is not the place to cut costs. These costumes need to be high quality." She'd taken responsibility for much of the labor herself to save money. "Your father gave me a budget and I've saved money in other areas, but I need your approval to shift some money around to cover the designs."

He took the paper and studied it critically. "How do I know these figures aren't going to balloon into more needed funds?"

She wanted to pull her hair, or maybe she should pull his. He looked so smug and self-satisfied. And gorgeous. Try as she might, Merry couldn't forget how hot he looked. She didn't understand why John would turn over the money handling to his son. She didn't think she could manage weeks of arguing with him. "I don't know. But I've planned and worked up spreadsheets, which I gave to your father as estimates. I'm working hard to stay as close to the budget as I can. Am I going to fight with you over every penny?"

She wanted to tell John that this wasn't part of the bargain. Yet at the same time, she was ready to go to war with Jake. She couldn't believe the man didn't have faith in his father. John was a shrewd businessman and he knew what he wanted and how to get it. Why couldn't his son see that?

"It's easy to overspend without even realizing it," Jake said, his eyes narrowing as though assessing her agitation. "This isn't like your former job where money isn't always an issue."

"Money's always an issue," she said with a laugh. Though she had to admit that with billions of dollars available an occasional overrun was hardly noticed. "You're not just buying Christmas this year, but Christmas for the next twenty years. The better the quality now, the less money spent later. Plus, you need me. Not only can I make what we need for today, but I can re-purpose all the props for the next twenty years and still make them relevant. You can't afford to be penny-wise and pound-foolish. It's better to spend now and maintain what we have than buy cheap year after year. Trust me, in the end all the props, costumes and decorations will cost more than you know. Plus, if you buy cheap now, people coming to the park will see the cheap decorations and think the rides aren't being maintained properly because we couldn't be bothered to get quality in the decorations."

His eyebrows went up at that statement.

She tried not to grin. She'd thought of something he hadn't. "Why do you think places like Chapman, Knotts Berry Farm, Disney and Six Flags thrive year after year?"

"Why don't you tell me?" he asked, sitting back and looking amused.

"Because they understand what the customer wants and they give it to them. That may be on a much grander scale than we can manage, but the principle is the same."

"All right," he said with a shrug. "I'm going to give

you this one. But I want to see a complete cost break-down of every penny you want to spend."

"I don't cut corners, Jake," she warned.

He nodded. "I understand."

She stared at him, trying to gauge the sincerity of his response. "I'll get the cost analysis and email it to you when I get back to my office."

After Merry left, Jake stood and went to the window to watch her walk along the path back to her office. He loved the way her hips swayed side to side as she walked. Occasionally she would stop and stare at a ride or an orange tree as though calculating what she would need to make the spot look Christmassy.

She had fire and passion, he'd give her that. And even he could see she knew what she was talking about, but for some reason he couldn't stop giving her a hard time. He'd wanted to see how she responded to obstacles, and the fact that she'd stood her ground and crafted a logical argument impressed him.

His phone rang and he glanced at the display. Agent Orange, aka Cecil Jones, his newest client, was calling. Jake sighed, trying to decide if he should answer or let the call go to voice mail. He wasn't certain he was up to dealing with this guy's issues. Jake and Cecil's lawyer had just done some fancy dancing with the IRS to fix the rapper's tax problems. Things were just starting to look up. The guy had money in the bank from all the music he'd written for commercials. He was never going to be a rap superstar, but he was making a damn good living if he didn't spend it all the way he wanted to.

"Cecil," Jake said. "What can I do for you?"

"I found a house," Cecil said without any other formality.

Cecil wanted a prestigious address. "Okay, tell me about it," Jake said, preparing himself for the coming fight.

"It's just a bungalow in Santa Monica."

"And how much is this bungalow going for."

"Six point five mil, man. I can afford that."

Jake sighed. "You can afford to buy the house, but don't you want to put some furniture in it, pay the utilities, put some food on the table for your kids?"

"But if I buy this house, it means I'm back on top, man. I can get out of this dump."

"Hollywood Hills is not a dump, Cecil," Jake said with another sigh.

"I'd be a lot closer to work," Cecil stated. "And I can live in a real house."

"You're living in a real house."

"I'm living with my mother."

"There's no shame in that. Your lawyer and I have worked really hard to get you back to the point where you could afford a house. But six point five million is way out of your price range. Buy something you can pay for outright and not have to worry about a house payment again."

"Jake, I want this house."

"Cecil, your children want to eat."

"The schools are good," Cecil said, changing the direction of his argument.

"And your kids are already going to one of the best magnet schools in the Hollywood Hills, and Cecil Jr. is in one of the best music programs."

"It's Santa Monica, man."

"Cecil, you're not talking me into this. I gave you a budget and that's what you're going to follow. The real estate agent found four houses in Hollywood Hills you

can afford. You can send your kids to great schools and
have your studio in your house. If you buy this house,
all you're going to have is a house. If you buy one of the
four houses in the Hollywood Hills I suggested you look
at, you'll have a life. So you have a decision to make."

"I want that house."

"Okay," Jake conceded. "You're telling me your ego
is more important than your future or your children's
future."

"That's not right, man."

"But it's the truth," Jake replied. *And everyone
laughed at me when I majored in finance with a minor
in psychology.* He heard a long-suffering sigh from the
other end of the phone and knew he'd won the argument. Cecil was a challenge, but he eventually accepted
Jake's arguments. He disconnected and Jake went back
to the window.

Merry was standing in front of the carousel. She tilted
her head from side to side. Jake watched her, running the
conversation with Cecil over again in his head. He'd managed Cecil without any problem. How come he couldn't
use the same skills with her? He should have been able
to talk her around to what he wanted, yet he'd tried to
intimidate her instead. He was used to working with difficult people, and she wasn't even trying to be difficult.
She was trying to do her job.

What the hell was wrong with him?

He stared at her, and for a moment he felt fifteen years
old again, watching her on TV, knowing she was way
beyond him and he would never get her no matter how
much he fantasized. How crazy was that? He'd been dealing with people like her for fifteen years, yet around her
he was completely clueless.

If he couldn't force her to his way of thinking, maybe

he should try flattery. Stroke her ego a bit. He pondered that idea for a minute. He was used to stroking fragile egos; he could do this.

He opened the door to his office and stepped out into the September heat. Heat waves shimmered from the sidewalks. After a glance at the thermometer, he started toward her. She had climbed onto the carousel and was studying one of the hand-carved animals. She sat down on a bench and opened her ever-present sketchbook.

"Did you know that *carousel* can also mean horse ballet?" Jake asked as he swung up on the platform. A glance at her sketchbook showed him she was drawing the horse. She frowned slightly as she added a flourish to the mane and then looked up at him.

"That's beautiful. I can see why a carousel could be called a horse ballet."

Jake stroked the horse she'd sketched. "All the horses on this carousel were hand carved in Germany in 1896." He smiled, remembering how much he'd loved riding the carousel as a child. "Want to see my favorite horse?" He held out his hand, and after a slight hesitation, she took it. He pulled her to her feet, led her around to the back and stopped in front of a white horse with a flowing blue mane. "When I was a kid, I used to pretend I was a knight of the Round Table and this was my trusty steed." Joy filled him as the pleasant memories returned. "And I would win the gold ring and present it to my princess."

"Really," she said, her dark eyes showing a touch of cynicism.

"You've never played make-believe?"

"Sure I did. Five days a week, eight hours a day for eleven years, until I outgrew the roles and decided to go to college."

"Why didn't you keep on acting? You were good."

"I got tired of playing the second banana. Then the roles started slowing down. I was never going to be lead-actress material. I had to make a life decision, and I decided to leave."

"Do you miss being catered to, fawned over and treated special, the way only actors are treated?"

She studied him. "No. That was not allowed in my mother's world."

"You mean you had a crazy mom manager."

"I wish," she said. "My mom wasn't my manager and she isn't crazy, but the one time I acted crazy, she snatched my butt home and wouldn't let me go back until I apologized to the entire crew. I even had to write a letter to Fred Chapman. The worst thing that ever happened to my career was when she had lunch with Ron Howard's mother at the studio."

"What do you mean?" Jake asked curiously.

"Apparently Ron Howard's mom didn't believe in children giving B.S. to their fellow actors. My mom didn't believe in it, either. I was taught to be respectful of others and consider them before I considered myself. And one tantrum from me shut the set down for almost a day until I apologized for my behavior."

"You mom sounds like one hell of a woman." He couldn't help a spurt of admiration.

"Her presence is a 'no madness' zone," Merry said in a rueful tone.

"If more of my clients had mothers like yours, I'd be out of business."

"What exactly do you do?" She ran her fingers down the neck of a zebra with flowers for a mane. She smiled as she stroked it.

"I'm in financial-crisis management. In other words, I help high-risk clients handle their finances when they can't do it themselves. Sometimes the court appoints me as their conservator. I take them in hand, heal their financial problems and get them out of trouble with creditors, the IRS or any other government agency they might owe money to."

"That's gotta be tough," she replied.

"No kidding."

"How do you get into something like that? I do see a need. A lot of the kids I worked with were broke by the time they were twenty. They could have used you. Especially Maddie." Her eyes turned sad.

"Maddie?"

"From *Maddie's Mad World*. Maddie Blake. She was the star and blew all her money on clothes she didn't need, gambling at the local casinos, living so lavishly she once had four expensive sports cars. You can only drive one car at a time, so why would anyone want four?"

"Her mother should have stopped her," he said, knowing how easy it was to be seduced by so much money and thinking it would be endless.

"Her mother makes Dina Lohan look like Mother Teresa."

He shrugged. "What about you?"

"I'm not wealthy," she replied. "But my mother was a smart cookie. She negotiated a lower up-front salary for me and higher residuals, so the money kept coming when the shows went into reruns. Thank you, God, for Hulu and Netflix."

"Your parents didn't raid your trust fund?"

She laughed. "They didn't need my money. My dad is an airline pilot and my mom is a successful artist."

"How do you invest your money to keep up a stream of income?" he asked. It wasn't any of his business, but he was curious. He so seldom worked with someone who understood the value of an investment portfolio.

She studied him as though trying to decide how much to tell him. "I have some real estate in Santa Ana, stocks and cash. My mother worked with someone like you to make sure I'd be secure the rest of my life as long as I don't get stupid and spend it all."

"So you really don't have to work if you don't want to?" And she was wise with her money. That made him feel better, knowing she wasn't after his father's money.

"I have a mortgage payment just like everyone else in the world. My residuals are nice to get, but not enough to pay it. Besides, I like working," she said, an almost defensive tone in her voice. "I'd go crazy if I didn't have something to do. I'm not the kind of person to sit around and twiddle my thumbs. What's with the third degree? I'm not skimming money from your father."

"Sorry. I really didn't mean to imply you were stealing from my dad."

"Yes, you did," she said tartly.

"I know he wants to make people happy. He's not in a business that's out to get other people. But I still have to make sure the money goes where it's supposed to go. That it's not frittered away on stupid things."

"I don't fritter money away on stupid things," she answered hotly. "My reputation is on the line. If any whisper of misappropriation of funds even gets started, I'll never get another job in the entertainment field. I'm not going to risk that. I love what I do. Even as far back at being on *Maddie's Mad World,* I used to rearrange the set to make it feel warmer, or more cozy, or just plain fun. Even then I knew if the acting didn't pan out, I'd go into set design."

"So you have no aspirations for a movie career?"

She shrugged. "If it was going to happen, it would have, but it didn't. One of the things I learned very early was that your fifteen minutes of fame is over pretty quick. And there's more to life than trying to relive that moment."

Damn, he couldn't find any chinks in her armor. In fact, knowing she was self-reliant and ethical gave him a small feeling of relief. But this was his father, and Jake still had to protect him. Since his mother's death, John had faltered a time or two with women who'd wanted to suck him dry. Jake had stepped in each time and exposed them for what they were.

"If you're worried about your legacy, you don't need to be. I'm not going to touch it. I'm just here to help your dad get this place back on its feet. It's a great place and has so much potential. It just needs a little more TLC." She stepped into the stirrup of a horse and sat down on the saddle. "Stop being a stodgy old banker and let's go for a ride." She grinned at him infectiously.

His stared at her for a moment. "Sure, why not?" He stepped across the platform to the center of the carousel, started the motor and turned on the music. As the motor warmed up, he found himself grinning. "Ready?" he asked over his shoulder.

"You bet," came her answer.

He put the motor in gear and the carousel began to turn, the music blasting out from the speakers. He grabbed a pole, pulled himself up and mounted the horse next to her. Her eyes were closed as she gripped the pole in front of her. Her horse went up and down, and she looked absolutely content.

Chapter 4

A knock sounded at the door to Merry's office, and a second later it flew open to reveal her sister, Noelle. Noelle Alcott was an inch taller and a year younger than Merry with a willowy frame, pixie-cut black hair and laughing brown eyes.

"I brought you a present," Noelle said, handing Merry a small glass bear wearing a Christmas hat.

"Is this your new line?" The little glass bear fit in the palm of Merry's hand. Noelle was a glass blower.

"Isn't it cute?" Noelle strolled around Merry's office, stopping to study each drawing hanging on the wall. "It's Santa Benny Bear."

Merry laughed. "Named after the park mascot."

"Listening to you talk about all this inspired me."

"We can sell these here. They'll walk out of the store."

"I'd rather they ran out of the store," Noelle said. She stopped in front of one drawing showcasing the old ghost-town buildings that housed local vendors and their products. Merry was giving it a facelift, and a construction crew was currently hammering away, making her plan into reality.

The buildings were currently in a long line, and Merry would have liked to move them around to create a more village-like feel, but that would be for another facelift.

"You want to see the park?" Merry asked, jumping down off her stool and turning off the gooseneck lamp that lit her worktable.

"That's why I'm here," Noelle said.

Merry handed her a large, floppy-brimmed sunhat and placed another one on her own head. September had turned into a scorcher, with bright cloudless skies and one-hundred-plus degrees and rising.

Merry had set up a three-part plan for the renovation of the park. Once it was open again, the second part would be to start planting trees for shade. Why the park had no shade trees, she didn't understand.

"How's the new boss?" Noelle asked as they stepped into the fierce sunshine.

"He is driving me insane," Merry said, trying to keep the frustration out of her voice. "He counts every penny I want to spend and then tells me I have to bring the job in for ten percent less. He questions every move I make. And he watches me."

Noelle's eyebrows rose. "You make him sound like a stalker."

"I think he follows me home." She led her sister toward the old ghost-town buildings. "Overall, I'm seven percent underbudget and things are getting done, but I have to justify every moment of my time when I'm here. And let me tell you, it's no fun."

She could hear the banging and hammering as they

approached the ghost town. A construction crew had begun extensive repairs on the roofs. "John is such a honey to work for, but Jacob is a tyrant."

"Tyrants can be tamed," Noelle said.

Merry's eyebrows went up. "Why should I bother?"

"I don't know. Maybe because you get a funny look on your face when you talk about him." Noelle's gaze was mischievous.

Merry opened the door to one of the buildings and led Noelle inside. The retail area was small and intimate. Ever since Noelle had asked about selling her glassware at the park, Merry had been thinking about which store would work for her. And she'd narrowed it down to two.

"What are you trying to say, sis?" Merry watched her sister study the room. She pulled a measuring tape out of her pocket and started to measure the room. She pulled a notebook out of her back pocket and marked down the length of each wall.

"Oh, nothing," Noelle replied. "I was just being sisterly, chatty, friendly."

"Why are you here again?"

Noelle laughed. "Because somebody needs to ruffle your little feathers."

"Consider my feathers ruffled."

"I've done my job. How much is this space going for? I like this one."

Merry could see that her mind was already figuring out the possibilities for showcasing her glassware to the best possible advantage. "Why do you want your own store? I thought you were doing well in the galleries." She took her phone out of her pocket and started snapping photos of the shop from every angle.

Noelle sighed. "Things have slowed down. So I'm doing smaller projects, knickknacks, jewelry...."

"Are things that bad?" Merry asked.

Noelle shrugged. "The little things are selling well. I'm working harder, but people are only spending money on little luxuries."

Noelle's glassware was museum quality. She'd even designed a garden of glass flowers and trees that echoed like musical chimes.

"But you've had a number of large commissions," Merry said, puzzled. "Didn't you design the atrium in one of the Las Vegas hotels?"

"I did, but it didn't result in more commissions. Lots of *oohs* and *ahhs,* but no more business. The money came from making miniature copies of the large flowers and selling those in the gift shops," Noelle said. She measured another wall and made some notes in her spiral notebook. "And that got me thinking about your park and maybe opening my own retail store. This way, I bypass the middleman. I can hire some people to work here and have more time to work in the studio."

"Let's talk to John, then," Merry said, stepping to the door and pulling it open.

Jake stood on the other side, one hand raised as though he'd been about to enter. "Jake," Merry said. "Did you need something?"

Noelle scooted past Merry, her gaze calculating as she studied Jake.

"Dad said you might have a renter for this unit. I came to check it out." He looked at Noelle questioningly. "And you must be...?"

Noelle held out her hand. "I'm Noelle, Merry's baby sister, though I'm only a year younger," she said with a grin. "You must be Jake."

He looked startled. "Nice to meet you."

"Funny, you don't look like Scrooge."

Merry glared at her sister. She wanted to die. How could Noelle say such a thing?

He laughed a little uneasily. "I see we've been sharing sister confidences."

"Which were supposed to be confidential," Merry said, seriously considering slapping her hand over Noelle's mouth.

Noelle waved her hand.

"What do you do?" Jake asked politely.

"I'm a blower," Noelle said with a grin.

Merry pinched the bridge of her nose. Her sister just loved to toss that one out to strangers.

"A what...?"

"Noelle's a glass blower," Merry said hastily.

"I don't think I've ever met a glassblower. I didn't even know there was such a thing," he replied. He cast a glance at Merry and she could see he was comparing her to her sister.

"So you're thinking about renting space," Jake said.

"Yes, I am," Noelle replied.

Jake tilted his head. "I'm trying to visualize this."

"I do glass jewelry, knickknacks like little glass flowers or for this park, I did a little Benny the Bear. It's in Merry's office."

His eyebrows went up. "Do those kinds of things sell?"

"I thought I'd theme my products to the park, like carousel horses, Benny the Bear, maybe orange paperweights, and some of my own jewelry creations. People want classy mementos, they don't want cheesy stuff."

Jake looked thoughtful. "I have an errand to run. Why not meet me in my office in thirty minutes?" He shook her hand and walked away.

Merry was stunned. Except for their afternoon on the carousel, she'd never seen him be this civil before.

Noelle studied him as he walked away. When he was out of sight, she pulled Merry back into the building and gave her sister a crushing hug. "He's a hottie. Wrapped a little too tight, but still hot."

"He's my boss, Noelle."

"Tell me you're not having inappropriate thoughts about him."

Merry's cheeks blazed with heat. "I don't have inappropriate thoughts."

"Then appropriate ones," Noelle said.

"Some days I want to stick a pickax in his head. That's the most appropriate thought I can come up with at the moment." Though at other times, she wanted to jump his bones. She didn't like that she had hot thoughts about him. "Besides, he's not my type."

Noelle burst out laughing. "Sweetie, he's every girl's type."

"Have at it, Noelle."

"I think not. Did you see the way he looked at you?"

"With scorn and distrust?"

"Girl, he *likes* you."

Merry rolled her eyes. "Oh, please. The only things that man likes are money, control and power. You should hear how he talks to his clients. Like they're five years old."

Noelle shook her head. She opened the door and stepped out into the hot September afternoon. "From what you've already told me, I suspect most of them act like five-year-olds."

"Come on, let's go back to my office. You'll probably want to take your little bear with you to show him what you can do."

Noelle just grinned. "By the time I get to his office, he'll already know. I can guarantee he'll check the internet first. But before I head over, I want to take a look at the carousel and get photos of the horses."

Merry closed the door to the shop and pointed her sister in the right direction. Noelle marched off, camera in hand.

Jake spent a few minutes looking up Noelle Alcott on the internet, preparing for her visit. What he discovered surprised him. She was quite the celebrated glass artist, having done several large commissions in Las Vegas and San Francisco. His cell phone rang. He glanced at the display and considered not answering it. He really didn't want to have a conversation with Annie Gray, but he had an obligation.

"What's wrong, Annie?" he asked, wondering if she was going to threaten him again, or try to talk him into another ten-thousand-dollar belt.

"Jake," Annie wailed. "I've been arrested and it's your fault. You need to come bail me out now."

"How is you being arrested my fault?"

"If you hadn't hijacked all my money, I could have paid for the shoes."

"Excuse me," Jake said, confused. "What are you talking about?"

"The stupid store manager says I stole them. I'm famous. He should have just given them to me."

Jake felt a laugh forming. "You shoplifted a pair of shoes."

"They were Louboutin shoes and they were on sale for only four thousand dollars."

Jake gulped. Four grand for a pair of shoes! This child was insane. "Again, what do you want me to do?"

"You go down to that store, pay the man for the shoes and get him to drop the charges."

Before he could answer, his phone buzzed, announcing another caller. "I'll call your mom," he said, and hung up in the middle of her wail.

"Hello, Gwen," he said to Annie's mother.

"I swear to God if you pay for those shoes or bail her out of jail, I will fire you," Gwen said swiftly.

"It's against my religion to pay four grand for a pair of shoes." Or ten grand for a belt.

"Thank you," Gwen said with a sigh. She started crying. "I don't know what happened to my daughter. She used to be sweet and thoughtful and caring. I blame my ex-husband. He didn't have the talent to live his rockstar dreams, so he pushed our daughter. She hates me."

Jake had met Annie's father. Mickey Gray was a feckless charmer with no thought for the future. He'd fought the court to gain conservatorship over his daughter, but the judge had his measure and appointed Jake instead. "Gwen, she just thinks she hates you, but there will be a point when she figures out you have her best interests at heart. Stay strong. You'll survive. She'll survive." *And I'll survive,* he thought.

"The best therapist I've ever had is you, an accountant."

"Are you sure you don't want me to bail her out?" he asked.

"Hell, yes, I'm sure. Let her spend the night in jail. She's in an isolated cell with a twenty-four-hour guard. She needs to think about what she did. I'd leave her there for a week if I could."

"If you don't have a lawyer, I can recommend someone who will be responsive to your needs as well as Annie's."

"Thanks, but I'm good," Gwen said with a sigh. "I'll talk to you later." She disconnected and Jake set his phone down.

A knock sounded at his door. Noelle Alcott opened it and peeked in. "Can I come in?"

"Sure."

She entered his office and sat down across from him. "You look like a man who's got troubles. I hope it's not my sister."

How did he answer a question like that? Yeah, Merry was a handful, but he'd never admit it to anyone. He rather enjoyed their confrontations. The memory of her on the carousel came back to him and he almost smiled. She had looked so beautiful sitting on her horse, with her eyes half closed and a tiny smile on her face.

"So what do you want to know about Merry?" Noelle asked as she settled herself in the chair.

"I'd rather know about you."

"I'm sure you and Google have already checked me out."

"Am I that transparent?" he asked, surprised.

"You're looking for a chink in Merry's armor, and you're hoping it's me."

Well, that put him in his place. She was a lot like her sister. The sassy apple didn't fall far from the tree, but she wasn't Merry. Merry was so vibrant; he didn't know enough about Noelle yet to even form an opinion, though he sensed she was very protective of her sister. "After the past few years of receiving big commissions for highly visible jobs, you're going to be happy doing knickknacks?"

"Harsh," she said. She set a glass bear on his desk. "And not totally accurate. I'm looking to expand my opportunities."

He sat back in his chair and studied her. "So what you're really saying is that big-commission work has fallen off."

"You got it. In this economy, how can you be surprised? You should know that 'pretty' is the first victim of a recession."

That fact that she could change direction in a heartbeat told him she was a pretty shrewd businessperson. Very much like Merry. He admired that ability in Merry.

"So about the retail space," she said.

"This park is hardly high-profile."

"Maybe, maybe not, but you are," she said. "I know you've already negotiated with two of your clients to perform in this park during the Christmas season. That's going to draw people in, and I'll be creating exactly the type of memorabilia that people are going to want to take home and place somewhere they can see to remember their experiences. And who knows? Maybe one of your high-profile clients will see something, buy it and take it home to show their friends, who then might just come and purchase their own."

Jake studied her. He hadn't thought of it that way. But she had. She was laying a foundation for her future, which he found very perceptive of her. She'd obviously given her idea a lot of thought. "I feel like I've been tag-teamed by the Alcott sisters."

Noelle laughed. "We have each other's backs. I'm delighted I'm getting the chance to work with my sister."

"You weren't in show business?"

She smiled. "Can't sing, can't dance, can't remember lines and have absolutely no acting talent. Our mother encouraged us to develop what we were good at and I was more the artist than Merry. Merry always wanted to be an actress. Set design was just her fallback position if acting didn't work out. And it didn't."

In his practice, Jake had encountered siblings who wanted their more famous family members to fail. Jealousy had been a constant with them. He didn't detect any jealousy in Noelle. She seemed genuinely pleased with her sister's success. He liked that.

"Is she unhappy?" Jake asked with a start. The thought of Merry being unhappy made him want to do something about it.

"Hell, no. She's thrilled."

"What would you have done if your glass art didn't work for you?"

"I have a degree in English. I like teaching."

Jake picked up the bear and saw his face reflected in the blue translucent side. "You did a good job capturing Benny's playfulness."

"Yeah, I had to work on that. It's hard making a grizzly bear look playful and not end up with it looking like Winnie the Pooh."

"Do you want to rent the store you were looking at?"

"Yeah, I do."

He pulled a contract out of the drawer. "You live in L.A. Why don't you want to get a retail space there?"

"For the price of what I'm getting here, I'd get a postage stamp in Los Angeles. More space, less money and the commute won't kill me. Besides, my studio is in Rancho Cucamonga, so I'm out here most days anyway."

Jake nodded. He gazed thoughtfully at the bear again and realized he liked it and wanted one for himself. He'd have his own Benny. "What will the price of this be?"

"I figured out it will cost around forty-five dollars. I'm going to work out a smaller one for twenty-seven and maybe one or two larger bears that will go for a hundred.

I also want to create some carousel horses, which will cost more since they'll be more labor intensive. I have to figure that out. I'll have jewelry to sell, which will go for anywhere from thirty to fifty dollars. And I'll do special projects for Christmas. I thought Benny in a Christmas hat or holding a wreath would be fun."

"I want everything involved with the art to be exclusive to the park."

"Of course," she replied. She pulled a notebook out of her pocket and started writing in it. "I want my lawyer to look over the contract. What's negotiable?"

She haggled cheerfully with him for a few minutes, and finally they agreed on the rent and some other negotiable items. He made notes on the contract and told her he would send it to her within a couple of days. After a firm handshake, she left.

He stood at the window and watched her stroll down the path back toward Merry's office. He'd had a plum opportunity to pump her for information about Merry, and he'd let the chance get away from him. He'd enjoyed talking to Noelle, but she made him feel like her big brother. He would never feel that way about Merry.

Candace Frenche walked around the staff performer, studying the elf costume she'd created. Wrapped around one wrist was a pink pincushion studded with straight pins. Merry sat in the first row of seats in the amphitheater with John Walters while Candace worked her magic.

Candace had had her start in costuming on *Maddie's Mad World.* From there she had moved on to various TV shows and into the movies. She and Merry had been friends since Merry's first day on the set. Merry had enjoyed watching Candace grow into the costume designer she was now.

Candace was a tall, slender woman with gleaming dark skin and amber-colored eyes. She wore her dark brown hair in a stylish ponytail at the back of her head with small clips on the sides to hold strays hairs in place. She was dramatic with a Naomi Campbell type of beauty.

"So you're saying we only have to buy one costume and it can be adjusted to fit whatever performer we have for the day."

"Exactly," Merry said. "There are hidden tracks inside with fabric ribbons that can be pulled tighter and loosened to fit whoever is wearing that particular costume for the day."

"Who knew?" John said. "How come this didn't exist when my kids were little? My wife wouldn't have made herself crazy trying to find clothes to fit them."

"What it means is that if you have ten different performers inside Benny the Bear's costume, you will only need one costume because it can be adjusted to fit."

"Wow," John said. "I'm impressed. You two are amazing." Then he snickered.

Merry grinned and turned back to watch. Candace had dismissed the elves and was now studying the carolers who would roam the park singing Christmas carols in Victorian-style costumes. The women's clothes were floor-length dresses in various colors and then men wore top hats and knee-length coats with old-style cravats tied into enormous bows beneath their chins.

The door to the amphitheater opened, throwing a flash of sunlight across the stage. Candace looked up, distracted and annoyed. Merry glanced back to find Jake bearing down on her.

He frowned at her as he sat down. He didn't look as though he was having a good day.

"So these are the costumes." Jake didn't sound enthused as he watched the parade of performers. Merry kept a blank face, but in her mind she was giving him the mental stink eye. She and John had been enjoying themselves and Jake was raining on their parade.

John gave his son an annoyed look. "Jake, be polite. Merry is working her butt off."

Jake's frown took on a tired edge. Merry was afraid to ask how the meeting had gone between him and Noelle in case that was the reason he was so irritated.

"What's got you so twisted up at the moment?" John asked.

"Sometimes I think my life is as crazy as some of my clients'," Jake replied.

"Having client issues?" John asked.

Jake just shook his head. "Whoever said finance was boring…" His voice trailed away.

"Maybe you need a vacation," John said.

Take one now, Merry thought. *Get out of my hair, make my life easier.* She turned back to the stage. Candace was pulling at the fabric of one of the women's skirts. She seemed to be muttering to herself, but Merry couldn't quite hear what she was saying.

Jake leaned forward, his elbows on his knees. "I guess I'm a little tired. But right now is no time for a vacation." He shot a meaningful look at Merry.

From the tone in his voice, Merry figured this was as close to an apology as she was going to get.

"I just got a call from Max. He's been Benny for the past two years, but he was accepted at a college in Ohio and he'll be leaving soon. We'll have to hire a new Benny. We'll have to buy another costume."

"Okay," John said, completely unperturbed. "We won't have to purchase a new costume. Merry was just explaining how there's all these hidden doodads and strings inside that make the costume one size fits all. It's Merry magic."

"I can't take credit for that. This is all Candace."

Candace had ushered the carolers off and was now motioning to Mrs. Claus. Merry smiled. Mrs. Claus's costume was Merry's favorite.

Jake made no comment as he watched Mrs. Claus prance around the stage.

"I don't know when," Merry said, "but at some point you have to trust me. I'm not in kindergarten like some of your clients. I'm twenty-nine. I'm responsible. I'm as careful with other people's money as I am with my own. And I wish you would treat me as though I'm adult."

"I trust lots of people. I trust them to be childish. I trust them to whine when things are inconvenient and I trust them to get away with everything they can. I just don't trust them with money."

Merry blew out an exasperated sigh. "The caliber of people you associate with must really depress you. Let me help you. I'll take you out to dinner. I'll even take you someplace cheap." Had she just asked him on a date? *Where is your brain, girl?*

Jake burst out laughing. "How cheap is cheap?"

"McDonald's has a dollar menu. But for you, I'd spring for something costing five, maybe even six bucks, easy. Drink included."

She could see by the way he stared at her he was looking for an answer.

"She's got you there, son," John said with a chuckle.

"I want good, cheap food that doesn't come from a restaurant with a drive-through window."

Oh, well, she could make this fun. "You drive a hard bargain. I know exactly the place."

His eyebrows went up. "Done."

Merry grinned. She was going to show him. "Okay, you're on."

Chapter 5

Jake parked in front of her house, a small bungalow in a quiet Pasadena neighborhood situated on a large lot. The house looked small from the outside, with huge hydrangeas flanking the sidewalk leading up to the shaded front porch. Large live oaks towered over the bungalow. A huge orange-colored cat sat on the first step, staring at him.

He walked up the pathway approaching the cat. The cat didn't even blink as he put one foot on the step. He walked up to the front door and almost fell in love with its old-fashioned rounded top and small stained glass window set at eye level.

He punched the doorbell and, after a moment, heard the sound of footsteps from inside. Merry threw open the door. The cat darted inside, gave a slight meow and disappeared down the hallway. Merry took one look at Jake and shook her head. "You're wearing a suit."

"We're going to dinner."

"A casual dinner," she said with a sigh.

She wore a stylish white sundress with red polka dots. The hem ended midway between thigh and knee, showing off her long, slender legs. The sleeveless dress displayed her toned arms. Her feet were decorated with expensive sandals that had ribbons that wound around her ankles. If not for the fact that he worked with so many fashion-conscious women, he would never have known they were Valentino. He caught a whiff of her perfume and inhaled the heady scent. He tried to identify it but couldn't. And he thought he knew his perfumes.

"Nice shoes," he said.

"I know. Shoes are my kryptonite. The secret is out. But if it makes you feel any better, I found the dress on sale at Saks at the year-end sale. Perfect for the beach." She tilted her head.

"You didn't say we were going to the beach."

"I said cheap. I thought we decided on the kind of cheap that doesn't include Hugo Boss suits and ties." She eyed him critically. "Lose the tie and hopefully no one will notice."

He found himself peering over her shoulder, trying to get a feel for her house. She raised her eyebrows. "Would you like to come in a moment and see my home? It has quite the history."

She opened the door wider and he walked inside, his shoes loud on her wood floor. The hallway spanned the center of the house. On his left was a medium-size living room decorated in blond-colored wood furniture that had a definite arts and crafts look to it.

"The house used to belong to Ernie Cordova."

"He was a singer. Did a string of Busby Berkeley musicals back in the thirties and forties. This house was party central. In fact, you are walking on floors that supported the weight of W.C. Fields, Cary Grant, Katherine Hepburn and Spencer Tracy."

He didn't want to be impressed, but he was. "That's quite a history." He'd expected a very different house from what she showed him.

He expected to find a house filled with clutter, with drawing materials everywhere. Instead, she showed him a tidy dining room and the kitchen. Each room was a masterpiece of arts and crafts simplicity, with elegant art deco Erté lithographs on the walls and a few canvases that she explained had been painted by her mother. Even her office was a surprise. He had thought it would be filled with tons of photos of herself and the awards she'd won. Instead, he found a couple of photos on one wall and two awards tucked away inside a bookcase.

"I've been in many of my clients' homes," he said as he looked around at the office, which had been tastefully decorated with wood panels, bookcases, a tilted drawing table with a gooseneck lamp and a tidy wooden desk. "They have photos of themselves everywhere." Especially Annie Gray, whose small condo was literally littered with her stuff. "Why not you?"

"That's my past," she said, touching the corner of a photo of her and her costars from *Maddie's Mad World.* "It's fun to remember my acting days, but I think the future is much more exciting. Every day is a mystery and a challenge."

He was dumfounded at her answer. "I don't know what to say."

"From what I see, you deal with the worst of celebrities. You wouldn't have a job if the majority of the people you deal with were financially responsible. Does that change your opinion of me?"

Every moment with her was a surprise. A surprise he found he liked. His own clients were so predictable and Merry was so charmingly unpredictable. Even if she was going to make him walk in the sand at the beach.

Usually he was right on the money with people. He could tell by just looking at them how financially strapped they were. Usually the more expensive their clothes, the more in debt they were.

Merry was so very different from the character she'd played on *Maddie's Mad World*. Chloe had been kooky and a bit naive. Merry was so different—more like the savvy girl next door. She was quick and smart, always ready with a comeback. Chloe had been easily led astray. Merry was focused and on task almost all the time. He was starting to like Merry the woman better than the Chloe he'd had a crush on. Chloe had been charming in her way, but Merry was devastatingly delightful.

She led him out onto the back patio to a long, narrow yard filled with a jungle that was taller than he. In the middle of the jungle he saw a pool, the blue water sparkling in the sun.

"You like the garden," he said.

"Actually, I like to swim. My gardener likes to garden." She led him down an overgrown path to the pool, which was more a lap pool than for playing in.

Again, he was surprised. She looked at her watch. "We'd better get going. You look like you're brooding, so let's go have some beach time." She turned back to the house.

He opened the door to his Mercedes sedan and she slid into the passenger seat.

"Where are we going?" he asked.

"Venice Beach," she answered.

"What's in Venice Beach?"

"The world's best-kept secret."

He pulled smoothly out onto the street and headed for the freeway. He liked the way she looked in his car with her cheerful dress and her long legs crossed neatly at the ankles. Her ponytail swayed gently as he turned onto the entry ramp. He caught another whiff of her subtle perfume.

"So tell me," he said as he merged into the freeway traffic, "what was it like being an actress?"

She tilted her head as she thought. "That's a broad question."

"Did you like being a child actress?" he said.

"All the time," she said. "I loved it. I loved the hard work, the energy. By the time you're six or seven you stop believing in make-believe, but as a child actress, I got to stay inside that make-believe world until I was almost eighteen."

"It doesn't seem to have stunted your growth in any way."

"My parents were very grounded, which was good for me. Because if I'd had crazy parents, I probably would have ended up crazy. One of the best things my mother did was value artistic expression, but she was still practical. She would never have abandoned us and run off to Tahiti to pursue her art. She might have made us all move with her, but she'd never do anything that put her art first. And that's what I learned. I could be an artist and still live in the real world. What about you? You grew up with an amusement park as your playground."

Jake found himself smiling. "It was fun. I could ride the carousel for as long as I wanted. But I never knew if my friends wanted to hang out with me because they liked me or because they wanted free tickets."

"I know exactly what you mean. It was easier to have friends in the business."

"Was your sister jealous?"

She turned to study him. "What's with the deep and personal here?"

"Just asking."

"Noelle had her own interests that my parents encouraged. She can draw and paint and sculpt and create exquisite glass sculptures. She can make something out of nothing."

"What about what you do? Your house is a show place."

"Say what you will, everything in that house is something I love, and the lucky part was that it all worked together."

Traffic was heavy for a Saturday. It seemed that, with the prolonged hundred-degree weather, everyone was heading for the beach. They fell into silence as Jake concentrated on driving. He thought about Merry and what her childhood had been like compared to his own. As a child, he'd loved the park, but he'd grown to resent it as it had consumed his father's time.

Not until he was an adult and graduated from college did he realize all the advantages the park had given him. It had paid for his education. He'd learned to deal with difficult people. He could operate every ride and even do some simple fixes when something broke down. He'd learned to handle money.

His father had made sure he could do everything, and after a while he'd realized the park was a family business even though he and his sister had chosen very different paths. He wondered if his father had been hurt by the direction his life had gone. If so, he'd never said a word.

Thinking back on his life, his father had subtly encouraged him to seek his own way.

He realized his father didn't want to retire. His father loved that park. He'd helped build it with his own hands; he'd put his soul into it. Which made Jake start thinking about his grandparents and how they must have felt when his father had decided to build the park instead of farming.

"You're frowning. What are you thinking about?" Merry asked.

"My father," he said. "He always encouraged me to go my own way, but I started wondering what he really wanted for me. I know he would have liked me to take over the park, but I didn't have any interest in it and neither did my sister."

"My parents weren't too thrilled about my acting. I had to do a lot of tap dancing and make a lot of promises to get my mom to take me to auditions."

"What kind of promises?"

"No grades lower than an A minus, and I had to sign a contract that I would go to college."

"You'd think your mother would support a daughter in the arts. After all, she's renowned for her stained glass."

"Yeah, with her degree in political science. My parents were the hedge-your-bets kind of people. After all, look how my acting career turned out."

"Are you unhappy with what you're doing?" he asked, wondering if his father had made a mistake hiring her.

"I love what I'm doing." She leaned toward him. "But don't tell anybody, I like set design a lot more than I ever liked acting."

He glanced at her, totally surprised. "I would never have known that."

"Acting is a lot of pressure. Pressure to remain thin,

pressure to look a certain way and everything I did was scrutinized. I couldn't take a lunch break at McDonald's without someone taking a photo. And it's even worse now with Twitter, Facebook and Instagram. Honestly, I do not miss the spotlight, but I do occasionally miss that feeling of being special. It's addictive. But long-term relationships are hard to maintain."

As they approached the beach, they exited the freeway and fell into a long line of cars snaking down the boulevard.

"Being a celebrity did not do many of my clients any favors."

"You have to realize that the second you become a commodity, people treat you differently. Some people don't tell you no, letting you have whatever you want whenever you want it as long as you're famous. The second you stop being famous, everything goes away, and a lot of people will start telling you no, and you don't know how to react to that. A case in point is Maddie. She was cute and perky as a child and everyone loved her, but the minute she blossomed, her career went away and she couldn't manage the change. A lot of child actors get lost and never recover. My parents kept me grounded, and every day I feel lucky."

"Are you saying you're lucky to have survived your career or not to have had a longer one?"

"Both," she said. "Turn right at the next light."

People walked along the sidewalks carrying picnic baskets and towels over their arms, wearing big-brimmed hats that shaded their faces. He could smell the salt in the air; seagulls floated overhead.

"Turn down that alley," she said.

"But there's no parking," he protested as he turned into an alley shaded by large palm trees swaying in the ocean breeze. Carports opened onto the alley. He glimpsed tiny yards. The salt smell of the ocean was stronger than before, and he knew they were a block, maybe two, from the beach and that this area was prime real estate.

She directed him to a covered carport halfway down the alley.

"We can't park here. This is private property," he said, though the thought of trying to find parking in a public lot would be daunting on a day like this.

"This is my grandparents' house. Trust me, we'll be fine, and at the same time I'll find you something to wear besides a black suit."

He parked his Mercedes in the carport and she jumped out of the car, a set of keys in her hand. "I come here all the time. They won't mind."

Inside, the cottage was small but tidy. Painted in soothing blues and grays, the furnishings were a little worn but comfortable. The rooms smelled a little musty, but Merry cranked open the windows and fresh air, along with the scent of some flower, blew in and freshened the room.

"Now," she said, hands on her hips as she studied him, "to find you something to wear."

"Nothing too loud." Visions of plaid shorts and a blaring orange shirt filled his head.

"My grandfather is very conservative."

"Then nothing too old man," he replied, thinking he would come out smelling like mothballs.

Merry laughed as she walked down a narrow hallway. He stepped into the small living room. Four overstuffed chairs skirted a coffee table and shared space with a baby grand piano that barely left any room to maneuver. Behind the piano, sliding doors opened onto a large patio so overgrown with bushes and flowers he thought it was a jungle. On top of the piano were dozens of photos in plain frames. He glanced through them and saw Merry and her sister in various stages of growth, from babyhood to college graduations.

"Jake," Merry called.

He stepped into the hall and she stood at the end in front of an open door. She held khaki shorts and a purple-and-yellow Hawaiian shirt.

"No on the shirt," Jake said.

"Come help me," she said.

He stepped toward her. At the end of the hallway, he glimpsed a bright kitchen that was large and comfortable, and he instantly knew that this room was the real gathering place in the house, with its modern appliances, granite countertops and island with stools situated around it. A fireplace in the corner was flanked by a small sofa and matching chairs.

He followed her into a small, cozy bedroom decorated in green with a fireplace that was shared with the kitchen and a large bed with a bench at the foot.

"Something in white," he said when she pulled out another Hawaiian shirt, only slightly less loud than the first one.

Merry laughed again. She pulled out a white, short-sleeved pullover and tossed it to him. "The bathroom is through there." She left, closing the door after her.

He didn't feel comfortable in such casual clothes, but he knew he'd start to broil in his black suit once he was out in the sun. He neatly hung his suit coat, shirt and pants over a small wooden valet in a corner of the bedroom and donned the clothes she'd given him.

When he walked back into the living room, she was rummaging in another closet, and finally pulled out what she was looking for. She handed him a pair of sandals that adjusted with Velcro.

"Better," she said, looking him up and down. "Now you won't stick out like a sore thumb."

The sandals were a little big, but he pulled the Velcro straps tight. This was not how he pictured himself. He'd never been a beach person, but he'd agreed to a party once, and even though he'd had fun, he hadn't much liked the sand that got into everything.

Despite the breeze, the boardwalk was hot. People on skateboards, wearing roller skates or just walking moved along it. Waves slapped against the sandy beach, the roar a pleasant background sound for the chatter of voices. A few surfers sat on their boards a couple of hundred feet out waiting for the next wave. He was surprised at the risk the surfers were taking. Two great white sharks had been caught recently, which was one of the reasons Jake didn't swim in the ocean. That, and he couldn't see what was under him. The movie *Jaws* had scared him enough to confine his swimming to the swim park.

Two dogs bounded through the surf chasing Frisbees. Shops lined the street facing the beach, and he noticed there was a preponderance of tattoo parlors.

She led him down the boardwalk, passing a Chinese restaurant, a dozen T-shirt stores, a couple of stores showcasing what his father called TTTS, or ticky-tacky tourist shit, and another two tattoo parlors. She stopped at a pathway between a tattoo parlor and a Thai restaurant.

"We're eating at a tattoo parlor!" he said.

"Get inked while you eat your shrimp tacos," was her flippant answer.

He couldn't help teasing her. "What makes you think I'm not inked? I deal with rock stars and rappers every day. I'm down."

She stopped to look at him, eyes narrowed. "Is that an invitation to rip your clothes off right here and see what I can find?"

"You wouldn't want to ruin your grandfather's clothes, would you?"

She led him down the tiny pathway into a courtyard-type garden with tables clustered around a fountain and striped umbrellas shading the tables. Two tables were occupied, the rest empty. She led him to an empty table covered in brown butcher paper and sat down.

He sat down opposite her. He couldn't ever remember eating at a restaurant where he seated himself.

A man came out with an apron wrapped around his waist, holding a wooden board with a small loaf of bread on it. He slapped the bread down on the table and opened his arms wide.

"Merry," the man cried. Merry jumped up and threw her arms around him. "I wondered when I'd see you again now that you are gainfully employed."

Seeing Merry in another man's arms sent an odd jolt of emotion through Jake. He wanted to rip Merry away from the other man.

Merry laughed and hugged the man back, then broke away. "Andrew Becket, meet Jake Walters. Jake, this is Andy."

Jake recognized the man immediately. He'd played Maddie's older brother on the show. He stood and shook hands with him. "Mr. Becket," he said formally.

Andy Becket was tall and slender with long, slim hands and a face that was smooth and handsome in the way Hollywood seemed to treasure. When he smiled, he had a small dimple at the bottom of his chin. His eyes were a deep, clear blue with eyebrows that curved up and out like angel wings.

"Call me Andy. Everyone does," Andrew Becket said. "Nice to meet you, Jake. Merry's told me a few things about you."

Nothing kind, Jake thought, but he simply smiled. "I'm sure she has."

"Do you have any food allergies?" Merry asked.

"No," Jake replied.

She turned to Andy. "Bring it on," she said with a laugh.

"The works?" Andy asked.

"Do you really need to ask?" Merry said in a teasing voice.

Jake wondered what he was getting into. Andy went back into the restaurant and returned a few seconds later with a bottle of wine, setting it on the table with two glasses. He opened the wine and poured a bit into a glass for Merry to sip and approve. He served them and left again.

"Why did you bring me here?" Jake asked, eyeing the glass of wine. He'd never dined before where the waiter didn't ask his wine preference.

"Two reasons," Merry replied. "The food is awesome, and I wanted to show you another child star who isn't on drugs or broke."

Jake had to admit that his job was to deal with spiraling-out-of-control has-beens or newcomers. He knew his view of the industry was jaundiced and Merry wanted to show him another side.

"The media tends to concentrate on the worst that can happen to a child actor and seldom covers the best that can happen. Being a successful adult isn't news."

"So Andy's a success story," she said. "Are you familiar with the Barbarossa Brewery?"

"I eat there on occasion," Jake admitted. The food was

excellent, but the real achievement was the thousand different brews it offered from all over the world.

"Andy opened the first one and built it into a national chain. I invested in his restaurants and when he sold them, I bought a house. Not only is he a terrific chef, but he's also not insane."

"I know there are a lot of sane former child stars out in the world. I even have a number of them as clients. I really don't think all of you are crazy."

"But you thought I was going to fleece your dad out of his money," she said in a sugary-sweet tone. "Have you changed your mind yet?"

"I'm on a date with you," he said.

"This is a date?" She laughed. "I didn't think you liked me enough to want to date me. I thought I was just introducing you to cheap, terrific food."

"Is this a trick question?" Maybe *date* wasn't the right word. He wanted to get to know her better.

"And here I hoped you just wanted to get to know me better, to see I wasn't crazy."

"I know you're not crazy." In the space of a few hours he'd learned a lot about her and was surprised at how normal she was. "But I think your childhood was kind of crazy."

"Yeah, but it was fun." She leaned an elbow on the table and cupped her chin with her palm. "I met a lot of celebrities and I could tell you Mel Gibson was a whole bucket full of different when I met him."

"That's very diplomatic," he said, considering his own dealings with the actor.

"And I had the most embarrassing moment of my life when I met LL Cool J. I went totally fan girl on the poor man. And, ironically, the few times I've run into him in the past fifteen years, he remembers and really likes to tease me about it."

"What happened?" he asked curiously.

She held up a hand. "Not a chance." She took a sip of her wine and then cut the bread, slathering butter all over it.

He liked the fact that she didn't protest the calories or make comments about her figure. She liked to eat.

Andy came out carrying a large pot. He was followed by a young girl, about twelve years old, holding extra napkins.

"Hi, Cora," Merry said.

The little girl dimpled. "Hi, Merry. I'm working today."

"I can see that. Don't let your dad work you too hard."

Cora giggled.

"Ready," Andy said.

"Lean back," Merry told Jake.

In the next instant, Andy upended the pot on the table and mussels, small lobster tails, crab claws, shrimp and clams intermingled with half ears of corn, red potatoes and chunks of sausage came out. Steam rose from the food as it settled on the brown butcher paper.

"This is called Pirate's Fare," Andy explained, one hand gesturing outward. "It's my interpretation of a southern seafood boil."

Jake didn't know what a southern seafood boil was, but he could imagine. He leaned over the food, breathing in the tantalizing aromas.

Cora handed Jake a bib with a huge red lobster printed on it, a lobster cracker and a long narrow, two-pronged seafood fork. She set a bowl of melted butter in front of him and a pile of the extra napkins.

"Enjoy, kids," Andy said, retreating back into the restaurant.

"Dig in," Merry said, reaching for a lobster tail, pulling the meat out and dipping it in the butter. She closed her eyes as she chewed, a look of total delight on her face.

Jake could only stare at the food, wondering where to start. He had never had a meal served to him like this before. He was used to being with celebrities who were in crisis mode. He'd eaten at some of the trendiest restaurants in Los Angeles and consumed the finest food, and to look at the untidy pile in front of him left him at a loss.

"Just dig in," Merry said again. "It's okay to use your hands." She reached for a piece of corn, dipped it in butter and started eating it in neat rows from side to side.

He watched her for a moment, delighting in the way she ate the corn and didn't seem to worry about her figure. He selected a crab leg, cracked it open and dug out the meat. The moment the succulent meat hit his tongue he was hooked. It seemed to melt on his tongue. The sweet, tangy flavor rivaled any crab he'd ever had in the past.

"This is really good," he said as a pile of shells built up on the side of the table.

"I knew you'd like it," Merry said with a satisfied smile on her face. "Though I think I'm about stuffed. Would you excuse me for a few minutes?"

He nodded, his mouth full of the tastiest shrimp he'd ever eaten. After she left, Andy came out wiping his hands on a towel tucked into his belt. He grasped a wineglass by the stem and filled it as he sat down next to Jake.

"What did you think of the food?" Andy asked, eyeing the pile of shells.

"Outstanding," Jake replied. "When did you have time to learn to cook?" Andy's touch with food was amazing.

"When I was eighteen I couldn't wait to get away from acting, to take control of my life."

"Not a good experience for you?" Jake thought about some of his clients, whose own childhoods had been horrifying. Some rose above their pasts but others sank under the nightmares.

Andy looked up from the glass of wine he held between his fingers. "Just because you're good at something doesn't mean you have to like it."

Jake understood exactly where Andy was coming from. He thrived on the challenges even though his clients irritated the hell out of him at times. His job wasn't so much about his clients but about cleaning up their financial problems, which was the part he loved. Every morning he woke up energized by the thought of the trials he'd have during the day.

"What about Merry?" Jake asked. He wiped his hands on a napkin and took a sip of wine. The wine was extremely good and just the right complement for the food.

"Merry was different. She had something a lot of us didn't have."

"And that was?"

"Sane parents." Andy twirled the wine around the glass and looked at the garnet depths, his slender face contemplative.

"You realize I'm a complete stranger, don't you?" Jake said, a little uncomfortable with the possible revelations to home.

"There isn't anything I'm going to reveal that you couldn't find on Google," Andy replied. "I always thought Merry would make the transition to adult actor, and she did try. She had the talent, the looks and the brains. She was a way better actress than Maddie. But Maddie was the star of the show and she used her power to get whatever she wanted. And Merry ended up getting pigeonholed as the perky best friend. When the show ended, Merry's acting career ended, too, though at the time she didn't know it."

"So she gave up."

Andy shrugged. "She explored other opportunities. And her karma kicked in and she landed in a great job, and look what happened to Maddie. She ended up in rehab four times."

"What eventually happened to Maddie?"

Andy leaned forward, amusement in his dark blue eyes. "Remember the stolen tow truck chase a few years back? It was all over the news."

Jake remembered. He remembered being royally annoyed that the media had gone into a frenzy over the stolen tow truck and the woman driver. He'd never forget his three hours on the 405, stuck in traffic while police helicopters circled overhead. "That woman was Maddie."

"Yup," Andy said with a nod. "She called everybody who'd ever been on the show with her from the tow truck telling them to watch the news, all the while being chased by police. Now, that was a wheelbarrow full of nuts. And I might have ended up the same way if not for Merry and her parents. When I turned eighteen, got control of what was left of my money and decided not to act anymore, my parents kicked me out and Merry's parents took me in. They helped me get into Le Cordon Bleu and invested in my restaurant."

Cora came out again. "Daddy, Mommy says it's time for you to come home. We need to get ready if we're surfing tomorrow."

"Okay, Cora. Tell Mommy we'll be home in an hour." he said. She nodded and turned around went back to the restaurant.

"Are you closing up for the night?" Jake realized he wasn't quite ready to leave yet. He loved the sound of the fountain, the soothing ripple of water down the sides of a cherub in the center. He loved the peacefulness. The other two couples had departed and he had the courtyard alone with Merry.

"No, I have a great night manager and she'll take care of the rest of the evening. The late crowd hasn't even started yet. Wait another hour and there'll be a line out to the sidewalk."

"Thanks for the experience," Jake said. "The food was terrific."

"You're welcome." He stood, pushed the chair under the table and then leaned toward Jake. "Merry is an amazing woman. You could do a lot worse."

He could see that Andy was deeply fond of Merry. "I'll keep that in mind."

"And thanks for dropping by. The boss has spoken and I have to head home."

Merry came back as Andy disappeared into the restaurant.

"Did you have a nice chat with Andy?" she asked as she picked up her wine and sipped it.

"How did you know?"

"He does that with every guy I bring here. He makes me go the bathroom for ten minutes so he can chat without me around to look disapproving."

Jake hadn't really volunteered anything about himself. Andy had seemed more focused on Merry. "I don't think he learned anything significant."

"Yeah, he did." She picked up a shrimp and peeled the shell away. She dipped it in butter and popped it into her mouth. "He's the brother I never wanted until he showed up. Now I'm stuck with him."

Jake kind of knew what she meant even though he didn't have a brother. "Do you keep in touch with a lot of your costars?"

"Yes. There are a lot of us who are members of M.A. That's Maddie Anonymous." She grinned, her eyes sparkling in the growing dusk.

Twinkling lights wound around the jungle of plants and palms made the courtyard look like an enchanted forest.

"Being on the show was difficult for you, wasn't it?" In his mind, the only images he had of Merry from the show were as the faithful friend, the go-to girl who cleaned up Maddie's messes so she could get the guy while the girlfriend stayed in the background. He wondered if that was why he had loved her character so much.

"There are stars who make things easy," Merry said. "And there are stars who don't. Maddie was one of the don'ts. She believed her own press and made sure we knew who was the star of the universe." Her thoughts seemed to go inward as though reliving her days on the set; then she sat up straight, her shoulders going back, and she smiled at Jake.

Jake noticed an odd feeling go through him. Her face was half in shadow, her eyes sparkling and her mouth smiling. Whatever those memories were, they were pleasant. And she looked wistful as she sipped the last of her wine.

"Let's walk on the beach," she said. "It's a beautiful evening. I don't want to end it."

They finished their wine and paid the bill. By the time Jake had guided Merry out to the street, night had completely fallen and the heat of the day was dissipating. He could see fog banks in the distance rolling toward the shore. Soon the fog would shroud everything. But for the moment, the sky was clear, the stars were twinkling and the moon was coming up over the horizon.

"Have you decided I'm not so bad?" Merry asked as she stood on the sand, pulling off her sandals. They dangled from her fingers as she started walking along the edge of the water.

The roar of the surf filled the air. The surfers were gone and so were most of the tourists. Up and down the boardwalk, stores were closing. Merry paused as a wave washed over her feet. In her red-and-white dress, with her hair blowing in the wind, she looked waiflike and so utterly delectable he wanted to...to kiss her. The idea startled him.

Jake removed her grandfather's sandals and stuffed them in a back pocket. He took her hand as they walked. "I've decided you're not evil incarnate."

She quirked her eyebrows at him, grinned. "I'm moving up in the world."

"I'm just trying to protect my old man." He felt such a huge responsibility for his father that sometimes it was overwhelming.

"I know that," she said gently. "So I'll cut you some slack, but I can't help having a little fun at your expense."

"That's not nice," Jake protested, and she laughed, throwing her head back, exposing her long, slender throat. Well, maybe he deserved that. Merry was not the kind of person who took prisoners.

The moon had risen over the water, casting its reflection across the waves. Seagulls had settled for the night on the pier. A brown pelican bobbed in the water.

"I'm not always nice, but it is the truth. Your dad is a wonderful guy who knows what he wants. He's living in a world where it's hard to be successful doing what you love to do." Another wave washed in and she danced through it, kicking up her feet, her dress billowing to show her legs. "Do you like what you do?"

"Love it," he replied without hesitation. He couldn't see himself doing anything else. The idea of creating order out of chaos had always been something he loved to do. He remembered when he'd been in first grade, he'd organized the library books that rested on a ledge by the window into alphabetical order. The teacher had been amused and after that gave Jake little jobs that helped keep the classroom tidy.

"Then why," Merry continued, "is it okay for you to do what you want to do and not your dad? If he falls on his butt and loses all his money, are you going to abandon him?"

Jake stopped, his toes digging into the wet sand, shocked at what she suggested. "Of course not," he said. "I would never abandon him. He's my father."

She brushed hair out of her eyes and stopped to look at him. "Then let the man do what he wants to do."

"But…" he said.

"Your father doesn't need you to be constantly questioning his orders. What he needs is for you to be a safety net. I think because he's older, you don't think he has any dreams anymore. That he's lived his life and he should go off somewhere and do nothing for the rest of his life."

He grabbed her arm and swung her around to face him. "I'm not a bad son," he said, suddenly angry at her suggestion. "I love my father."

"I never said you were a bad son," she replied. The breeze stirred her hair, and the moon was reflected in her eyes. "But you smother him. You're overly cautious. Sometimes when I see you two together you act like the parent, and you treat him like he's nothing but a naughty child."

"I do not," Jake said, furious at her suggestion.

"Yeah, you do," she said. "I think it's quite sweet that you love your father so much, but trust me, your dad has all his marbles. You need to back off a little bit. Stop second-guessing him. Let him do what he loves to do."

"I think we should be heading home," he said abruptly. He didn't want to continue this conversation. She had no right to tell him how to take care of his father.

"Fine," she replied, stalking back up the beach to the boardwalk. She sat on a bench, brushed the sand off her feet and put her sandals back on. He did the same, feeling her chilly silence as an indictment against him.

In stony silence, they headed back to her grandparents' home. She told him to just collect his clothes and return her grandfather's beachwear another time.

He drove her home in silence, replaying their conversation on the beach over and over again. Was he trying to be his father's parent? Was he trying to keep his father from living his dream? Jake didn't think so; he just didn't want his father to make foolish decisions, and renovating the park seemed imprudent to Jake.

Once parked in her driveway, he jumped out, ran around the car and opened the door before she could. She stood and stared up at him, the streetlights casting deep shadows over her face.

"Thank you. I did have a lovely time." She stood on tiptoe to kiss him on the cheek.

"Oh, no," he said. "This was a real date, and I need a real kiss."

Chapter 6

His arms slid around her and Merry stood still. He was the enemy, and he made her life difficult. Did he deserve a kiss? As much as she wanted to kiss him, she couldn't. Tingling pleasure coursed through her. Her skin was on fire.

A second later, she pushed him away and held up her finger. "We are not going there," she warned. She stepped back, opened the door and walked into her house, slamming the door behind her. She leaned against it and listened, questioning her sanity. She heard a step, then another and finally the car door slammed and he started the engine. A second later she heard his car back out of her driveway.

She let out a pent-up breath. "What the hell am I thinking?" She stormed down the hallway to her bedroom. Her cat, Caesar, lay curled up on her bed. She sat down, pulled him into her lap and buried her face against him. "I wanted to do a bad, bad thing," she whispered. The cat yawned. "I can't get involved with this man." The cat struggled out of her arms and sat down, lifting one leg and started to clean himself. "Really? I'm having emotional issues and all you can think about is cleaning your business. Dude, you're supposed to be here for my emotional needs. That's what the lady at the shelter said. You're not doing your job."

The cat looked up at her, then jumped off the bed and walked out the door toward the kitchen.

"I took you out of that shelter, Caesar, I can take you back," she yelled.

She covered her face with her hands, reliving the moment, the almost touch of his lips on hers, the intense look on his face, the naked desire in his eyes.

She fished her phone out of her purse and dialed her sister. When Noelle answered, Merry said, "You know that cat you made me get? He sucks as a companion."

"What's going on?" Noelle asked.

"I'm having a crisis and Caesar is emotionally unavailable to me."

"You are not calling me about your cat, are you?"

"I wanted to kiss him."

"I've seen you kiss your cat all the time," Noelle said with an indulgent sigh.

Merry closed her eyes. "Not the cat. Jake Walters."

Silence sounded on the other end of the phone.

"Noelle, are you still there?" Merry asked, alarmed at her sister's silence.

Then Noelle giggled. The giggle burst into a laugh and the laugh rose in volume. When she had calmed down, Noelle said, "Wait a minute. You called me after you talked to your cat. You value your cat's advice over mine. I think I'll hang up."

"No, no, no," Merry moaned. "I'm having a crisis and you're feeling competitive with my cat."

"Just giving you a hard time, big sis," Noelle said, before she started laughing again.

"Stop laughing at me," Merry demanded.

Noelle finally managed to stop giggling. "You never let me have any fun."

"When you were sixteen, I got you backstage passes to the Black Eyed Peas concert. I know you had fun there."

"That was nine years ago," Noelle protested.

"I'm still rollin' on it. You should be, too."

"So you kissed him. How did that happen?"

Merry closed her eyes. "We really didn't kiss. I ducked, pushed him away and ran into the house. Then I cried on Caesar, and he just walked away."

"I repeat, you called me after your cat turned you down. What does that say about our relationship?"

"That we're sisters." Merry fell back and lay on the bed, staring at the ceiling, phone pressed tight to her ear.

"In my opinion, you should have just kissed him."

"I can't kiss him. His father's a nice man."

"What does his father have to do with it?" Noelle said.

"I don't know. Jake makes me insane. I have to justify every breath I take. I have to count pennies like they're made of solid gold." She hated the detail work he made her do. She understood it was necessary, but she felt she was doing more accounting than being creative.

"We've had this conversation before," Noelle said.

"That was before I almost kissed him," Merry replied.

"You're attracted to him. I can tell," Noelle said.

"I don't want to be." Merry closed her eyes. How was she going to get through the next months?

"Why were you two together on a Saturday?"

"I took him to Andy's," Merry admitted.

"You took Jake Walters to Andy's? You never take dates to Andy's unless you want Andy's approval."

Merry pinched the bridge of her nose. Taking Jake to meet Andy had been a big mistake. She wasn't even certain why she'd done it. "With all his financial oversight, I wanted to show him I was fiscally responsible and still capable of having a good time."

"Right," Noelle said.

"You're laughing at me again," Merry complained. She didn't understand why her sister was getting so much enjoyment out of her predicament.

"No, I'm not. But...if you want to get me backstage passes to the Pink concert, I could be persuaded to act a little more serious."

Merry started to laugh. "Blackmail. Is that all I am to you? Free concert tickets?"

"And movie premieres," Noelle said. "Sis, you have always been so focused on your career. I've never known you to be so distracted by a man before."

"What are you talking about?"

"You have never been particularly easy on the men you've dated."

"I'm nice," Merry said.

"You may be nice, but you don't put up with their crap, which is why you've reached the age of twenty-nine without any husband prospects on the horizon."

"You're twenty-eight and unmarried."

"I know I'm twenty-eight and unmarried, but I have three husband prospects on the horizon."

"You do?" Merry asked in surprise. "This is the first I've heard of it."

"There's the pool boy and the landscape man. And I recently met this killer plumber who unplugged my toilet. He even smelled good, like the commercials on the radio for the smell-good plumbers."

Now Merry knew her sister was just teasing her. "You like your men like you like your dinners—takeout. Eat, drink and be merry, for tomorrow you get put back in the ocean."

"At least I'm having fun," Noelle said. "On Monday when you go to work, pretend like nothing happened."

Merry didn't think it would be that easy. Jake Walters was not the kind of man to pretend. She disconnected and sat in the window seat of her bedroom, staring out over the pool. Caesar was playing jungle kitty in the wisteria, blending into the foliage as he eyed the empty hummingbird nest. The mommy hummingbird had placed the nest carefully, and every spring Caesar was a very frustrated cat.

How was she going to pretend nothing had happened? She could ignore him. That probably wouldn't work because he'd want her weekly expense report first thing Monday. She could call in sick and just stay home. No, that wouldn't work, either. That was the wimp way out. Besides, she had too little time, and she'd just started the construction of Santa's North Pole in the water-park area. She could distract him. She could pretend that she kissed her coworkers every day. That could work. Actors were very tactile and always hands-on. Or she could just slough it off as a mistake, but in the back of her mind she knew it wasn't. She'd wanted to kiss him for a long time.

She covered her face with her hands. What had she done? Why had she even agreed to take him out to dinner on the cheap? She was an idiot. Jake Walters was gorgeous. He was the hottest, most handsome man she'd met in years. And she wanted more than a kiss.

* * *

Jake stood at the window of his office, watching for Merry. He glanced at his watch again. She was running late and he felt a moment of anxiety. Was she okay? Had she been in an accident? Traffic had been horrendous this morning, with a number of accidents that had slowed the freeways to a crawl.

He pulled his cell phone out of his pocket and clicked through to her phone number. His finger hovered over the call button, but then he shoved the phone back in his pocket.

What had he done? He'd almost kissed her. If she hadn't pulled away, they would have engaged in a total lip-lock. Just the thought of the scent of her skin, the softness of her breath on his cheek, sent his pulse into overdrive.

He'd wanted to break his number-one rule: don't get involved with people in the entertainment field. They were too high maintenance, too flighty, with egos that bordered on the divine. And here he was lusting after an actress. No, he couldn't have that. Even though she wasn't in front of the cameras anymore, she was still part of the business. And she was so tempting. The temptation to kiss her and keep kissing her wouldn't go away.

He glanced at his watch again. Usually she was so punctual, so eager to be checking on her projects.

The sound of hammering reached him. The park had taken on a new look. Even he could see how festive it was becoming. He hadn't realized how drab it was. Merry was breathing new life into the park. New life into him. And that confused him.

He didn't like being confused. Usually he knew exactly what he wanted, where he was going, what he was doing. He'd set goals that he intended to accomplish by the time he was fifty. He wanted his house paid off, enough money in his savings and his IRA to keep himself comfortable. Then he was going to retire and travel the world. He would find himself a wife to share the adventures with and maybe have a kid or two. He would take on part-time work just to keep himself occupied, but nothing like the load he carried now. He had his whole life carefully planned out. Merry Alcott was not in his plan, and he refused to make adjustments.

His phone rang. For a second he hoped it was Merry, but it was Calvin Mayweather. "Hi, Calvin," Jake said. Calvin had been his client for almost ten years and was one of the sane ones.

"I'm glad I caught you, Jake. I just wanted to let you know my daughter was accepted at the UC Davis veterinary school." Calvin's voice held an edge of panic. "What am I going to do?"

Jake wanted to laugh. "We talked about this. First off, you're going to stop panicking and take a breath." When Jake had taken Calvin as a client, he'd had a boatload of debt and not a lot of income. Jake had reorganized his finances and found a whole lot of money Calvin didn't even know he had. And then he'd helped Calvin invest it, and suddenly Calvin was big again and selling his music rather than recording.

"I can't tell my baby no," Calvin said.

"Calvin, this is what we're going to do. I've been planning for this for the past four years and I showed you how we were to accomplish this."

"I know, but veterinary school is so expensive," Calvin said, worry evident in his tone.

"I got it. You have enough money set aside. Stop worrying. She's going to be an amazing vet."

Calvin chuckled. "She wants to be the vet to the stars."

"You've got the contacts. I don't think that's going to be a problem."

"When you first took me on as a client, I resented you every second telling me how to manage my money and treating me like I was five years old."

"I never treated you like you were five years old," Jake said.

"But I felt like it. And now I can't thank you enough. Telling my baby girl she couldn't have her dream was giving me nightmares."

"We'll get through this," Jake said.

Merry's Prius suddenly turned into the parking lot.

"Listen, Calvin, I've got to go, but let's talk about this more later. In the meantime, try not to get stressed. I'll help you work this out." Jake disconnected as he walked to the door and stepped out into the hot September morning. It was going to be another scorcher.

Merry opened the trunk of the car as Jake approached.

"I was starting to worry," Jake said.

Merry glanced up at him, startled. "I'm not wasting your money, if that's what you're worried about. I'll put in my full eight-hour day."

"I didn't…didn't mean it that way."

"What did you mean?" She hoisted several garment bags out of the trunk and over one arm.

"I meant that traffic was bad and there were a lot of accidents…."

"You were worried about me. The fact that we almost shared a kiss doesn't mean anything. You don't need to worry about me. And for your information, I just stopped to get some of the finished costumes for the Santa display." She walked away, her head held high while Jake wondered what the heck had just happened.

"That was quite a scene," Jake's father said.

Jake whirled around. His father leaned against the bumper of his truck, feet crossed at the ankles, his arms crossed over his chest. "You saw that?"

"I see everything, especially when the whole thing goes down right in front of me." He uncrossed his arms and stood up.

The wind had picked up, blowing sand across the parking lot. Jake fell into step next to his dad as they walked toward the park entrance.

"Having lady problems, are you?" John said with a low chuckle. "Somehow I thought when you got to this age with experience under your belt, this would be a thing of the past."

Jake didn't say anything. He felt as if he was back in high school again, drooling over Merry's character Chloe and wanting to fix her problems. "Are you enjoying this?"

"Yes," his father said.

"So you decided to give me some advice."

"I think you need it, so I can enjoy it more."

Jaw clenched, teeth grinding, Jake almost growled. "I don't need your advice."

"If you think so, but Merry isn't one of your clients. You can't treat her like one."

"I wasn't," Jake objected.

"Sure you are," John continued unperturbed. "She's an intelligent, clever, fiscally responsible woman and you keep hoping she'll screw up so you can rescue her like you rescue all your other clients. That isn't going to work with her. Some women don't need you to be their hero."

By virtue of his job, he was the knight in shining armor who rode in to save the day, to save the damsel in distress. He didn't think of himself as a knight, but he loved the feeling he had when everything went right for his clients. They needed him. He stopped walking as he rolled the thoughts over in his mind.

"Figured it out, did you?" John said. "Merry doesn't need you to fix anything, and that's what bothers you about her."

What did that say about his relationship with women? He thought about the women he'd dated. They were all professional in some way, but there was always something about them that needed rescuing. Something that he could fix for them.

"So what do I do?"

"You like her, don't you?"

Merry had come out of her office and was talking with the foreman of the construction crew. She held a drawing pad in her hand and pointed at it as she talked.

"What's not to like?" Jake mused as the foreman nodded at Merry's instructions. Then he turned and walked away, speaking into his walkie-talkie as he went.

John simply laughed and said, "You need to rethink how to work with Merry. Figure it out fast, son. She's going to make this park a success in a way it's never been before, and someone else is going to see what she's done, make her an offer she can't refuse and she'll be gone because she'll be comparing the way you've treated her with the future job. You may come up lacking. I need her to stay."

"Are you asking me to seduce her so she'll stay here?"

"I'm asking you to ease up on your suspicions. Give her some room and let her do her job. Amazingly enough, Jake, there are people in this world who know how to do that." John tucked his hands in his pockets and walked away, leaving Jake standing in the middle of the path with the wind whipping the flags on their poles and snapping the cables against the steel.

Merry had disappeared, but he caught a glimpse of her as she headed toward the water park. He followed her, wondering what he was going to say when he caught up to her.

He found Merry standing in front of a display of large wood boxes. The boxes had been painted in Christmas green and red. Merry attached a large red plastic bow to one of the boxes and stood back to look at it.

He watched her for a moment as she worked. She shifted the boxes back and forth until she finally settled on an arrangement she liked. She reached out toward a canvas-covered statute on a dolly and wheeled it into position. As she wrestled the statue off the dolly, Jake stepped up to help her.

"Where do you want it?" he asked as she pushed the dolly away with her foot.

She tilted her head one way and then another. "Right there."

After he'd positioned the statue, she pulled the canvas off to reveal a large nutcracker.

"We need to call a truce," Jake said when the nutcracker was in the position she wanted. His father had been right.

Her eyebrows rose. "Are we going to bury the hatchet?"

"Yes. Listen, I want this park to be great for my dad. It's what he wants. It's important to him, so it has to be important to me. And he thinks you're the one who's going to save this."

"How is that calling a truce?"

"My dad is sixty-seven years old and he has always had a blind spot where this park in concerned. His father was rabidly against building it, but my dad did it anyway. My grandparents thought the park was nothing but a black hole sucking money that they felt belonged to them, and not one person thought my father would succeed. My grandparents thought they would die destitute after the years they'd lavished on the orange groves. But they didn't, and my dad did everything right. I don't want to be like my grandfather and make the renovations into a war, but I have to watch the money. I have to protect my dad even though he doesn't think he needs protecting."

"I get it," Merry said quietly. "Your dad's a dreamer. I understand exactly how he feels. I'm not going to waste the money. I'm not going to create frivolous things. I understand the bottom line. I have to do my job. I'm bringing John's dreams to life. Doctors, chemists and plumbers make existence possible, but artists, singers and actors make life worth living. And sometimes there's a price to pay for that."

John knew exactly what she meant. She might understand the creativity of the artist, but he saw the unsavory side. "I don't want my dad's dream to kill him."

"That's not your choice," Merry said gently.

"I still have to protect him."

"You're right, you do. But not to the point where you stifle him, where you stifle me."

Jake ran a hand across his face, his eyes closed. He felt a hand on his arm.

"Jake," Merry said, "I understand about disappointment, about losing. I spent years in the shadow of a diva, but there was a time when I realized I wasn't going to have the career I wanted. It was a major blow to my self-esteem. I found something else I loved as much."

He held his hand out. "Truce."

She shook his hand. "Truce."

Merry drew her hand back and searched his face. No matter what type of truce he offered her, it would be an uneasy one. She backed away. "Since we're burying the hatchet, I wanted to talk to you about getting some star power for our opening weekend. We're going to be competing with Black Friday shopping and Cyber Saturday, or whatever."

"Cyber Monday," he answered absently.

"We're going to need a draw."

"Did you have someone in mind?"

"You're the music man. Who do you know who would do a show for cheap but will bring in the crowds?"

He gazed at her thoughtfully, running through his list of clients in his head. "We'd want someone who'll put on a family-friendly performance, who can be professional, and you're coming to me looking for a draw."

"It's a win-win situation," she said. "You're here, you have the contacts." She had contacts, too, but she didn't want to fall back on them unless he didn't want to cooperate. "Besides, I already got the carolers. You get the headliner."

"Carolers!"

"The group that performs at the Dickens festival in downtown Riverside every February. They're very good and they're working for free."

"As in no money changing hands?" he asked, looking suspicious.

"Well—" she squirmed a little "—not totally free. But they're willing to perform in exchange for yearly passes to the park. I know you're out the money for the passes, but they'll spend money on food when they're here. Why not promise yearly passes to the headliner?"

He laughed at her. "You have really, really been thinking about this, haven't you?"

"Yeah," she replied. She'd worked hard to figure out ways to save money, and offering yearly passes in exchange for free labor or reduced labor costs had been one of them. John had approved.

"I need to think about this," he said.

"All you have to do is get one good act to show and others will follow. And if they're good enough, people will start putting this park on their summer agenda. In fact, I think we should have summer concerts like the more well-known parks. There's a lot of potential here," she said, swinging her hand to encompass the park. Her knuckles hit the nutcracker and it wobbled.

"Don't you think my dad thought about the potential?" he asked curiously.

"No, he didn't think about diversification." She knew John had some idea of where the park needed to go, but he didn't know which direction to take. "There's a lot to work with here. You have the rides, the water park, the go-karts and a small amphitheater that isn't really being utilized."

"It's too small for big acts," he replied.

"That doesn't mean we shouldn't use it," she said. "And it's not too small, it's intimate. One of my favorite shows was *MTV Unplugged*. And that's what you can do. The amphitheater is perfect for acoustic music, and I'll bet we can get bigger names than you think we can. Do you know what tweens would pay to see Justin Bieber unplugged? We could get him."

"He's not one of my clients,"

"That's not a problem. I spent a whole summer at the Pasadena Playhouse working for free. And my name on the marquee was enough to bring people in. And I did it just to prove that I could. You appeal to these people the right way, you'll get them here dirt cheap."

"That leaves out my clients," he said with a wry laugh. "They hire me because they don't have any money."

She held up her hand. "LL Cool J's career was revived on *MTV Unplugged.* And look at him now. He still produces music and stars on a highly rated TV show. Just think about it."

"I'll think about it," he promised.

She glanced at her watch. "I've got to go. I have an appointment with a woman who wants to open a bakery here that specializes in Russian food." She walked away, thinking how thrilled she was to have had an open conversation with him, considering the almost kiss. Her sister was right—act as though nothing had happened.

Chapter 7

During the morning, the wind increased until it was practically howling, and Merry started to panic. The weatherman had said it would be a mild windstorm, but this was changing rapidly into something stronger. Most of the displays hadn't been secured yet because she was still playing with the arrangements. And now the wind was moving them around as if they were nothing.

She raced across the pathway to John's office, and the wind was strong enough to practically blow her inside. She fell inside to find John standing at his window, looking at the flagpoles.

"This is the earliest Santa Ana we've ever had," John said.

"It's going to blow my displays all over the park."

"Get the construction crew together and we'll take everything to storage."

"I don't think the storage area is big enough."

"Then we'll pack things into the empty retail spaces."

Merry opened the door and ran into Jake. The wind pushed him into her and she flew back. "We need to get all the displays into storage areas or they'll be damaged by the wind."

"I'll get the construction crew started on it," Jake said.

Merry simply nodded as she ran down the path to the go-kart track, a little surprised that Jake would pitch in so readily. She couldn't think about Jake now. Her life was being blown away. Generally Santa Ana windstorms started in late October. She'd figured she had a couple more weeks before the first storm and enough time to get the displays secured.

The wind whipped her hair around her face and she reached into her pocket for a hair tie to secure it. She picked up the smaller wooden boxes, headed to the row of empty retail stores and set the boxes down in the first one. She ran back for more. Ribbons from a display flew past her. She chased them, but the wind was too strong. She rounded a corner and found Jake with a dolly piled high. He'd caught the ribbons and held them in his hand. He grinned at her and held them out, presenting them to her like a conquering hero. Merry laughed because chasing those ribbons had been silly and he'd been sweet to catch them for her.

"Thank you," she said.

"You're welcome," he replied as he turned back to push the dolly toward one of the retail stores.

The wind caught the top box and flung it away. It landed hard on the concrete path and broke into pieces. Merry felt tears start, a feeling of defeat settling over her like a mantle of doom.

"It's nothing we can't fix," Jake said as he wrestled

the broken pieces back to the dolly and held them down with his hand as he started pushing.

"I know you're right, and tomorrow I'll agree with you, but right now I feel beaten." She opened the door to one of the stores and he pushed the dolly inside, out of the wind.

"Okay," he said as he started unloading the boxes. When the dolly was empty, she held the door open for him. Once outside, he stopped and sniffed.

"Do you smell smoke?" he asked, raising a hand to shade his eyes as he scanned the blue sky.

"Fire," she said. She didn't see any smoke. The sky was a deep cloudless blue. The wind had shuttled the smog out to sea.

"Not close," he said, sniffing again.

Fire was always a worry for Southern California. Merry's father had once joked that California's four seasons were fire, wind, drought and mudslides. "I'll check the news and find out where it is," she said. The park was vulnerable to fire since it was smack dab in the middle of country surrounded by dry scrub brush, grass turned brown from the summer heat and rolling hills with the kind of conditions just right for spontaneous combustion.

She ran back to her office and turned on the news. Fortunately the fire was about seven miles east and a couple of miles north of the park. They were in no danger, but still she felt a slither of fear run through her. She'd seen the devastation a fire could leave behind. Andy had lived in the foothills behind the studio and had lost his home twice to fire before he'd moved to the beach to be nearer to his restaurant.

"We're safe," she told Jake when she sought him out a few moments later.

He nodded. The construction crew had brought the

last of the displays inside and had gone out to the retail area to pick up the roof shingles that littered the yard.

Merry could see the damage. Tears prickled in her eyes. So much work gone in just a few hours. She should have secured the displays. She should have known. How could she have been so careless?

Jake put an arm around her. There was sympathy in his eyes. "I said we can rebuild. Nothing had been so damaged it can't be repaired."

"It's the loss of time," Merry said. She felt comforted by his arm around her, but the image of their almost kiss haunted her. "And it's going to blow my budget."

"You've come in underbudget on almost every project. You have a few dollars here and there to use for the repairs until the insurance company pays."

"You have insurance!"

"Of course we have insurance," Jake said. "But it may not come through by the time we need it."

She brushed her tears away. She could do this. "Tomorrow I'll get back on that horse, but today I think I'll just go home and cry in my beer."

"Don't do that. Come to the Queen's Knickers with me and you can cry in their beer. They have the best fish and chips in California."

"Are you asking me out on a date?"

"No, I'm taking you drinking."

"Okay. I didn't want to have to tell my sister you're taking me out to a pub named the Queen's Knickers."

"Do you and your sister talk about me?"

"Not in a nice way," she answered, unable to resist teasing him.

"And this 'not in a nice way' consists of what?"

She tilted her head at him, suddenly feeling lighter

and happier. "I moan about what a penny-pinching miser you are."

He gazed at her thoughtfully for a few moments. "Then maybe I need to give you nicer things to talk about."

"If this night works out, I doubt I'll remember anything."

He chuckled. "I'd better get you a hotel room ahead of time."

"I'll get a room at the Mission Inn. If I'm going to have a hangover, I'm going to have one in a nice place."

"Considering that the Queen's Knickers is across the street, you won't have far to fall."

She laughed. "It's a date. I mean, a nondate. I mean, a drinking date. Scratch all that."

"I'll meet you in your office at five. I need to call the insurance people and find out how to get the ball rolling."

Merry grinned. She walked back to her office, looking forward to her nondate with Jake.

Merry loved the Queen's Knickers the moment she walked in. The huge bar was paneled in wood, with dark wood floors and royal memorabilia hanging on all the walls. A huge portrait of Her Majesty, Queen Elizabeth of England, hung over the fireplace, a pint in her hand.

The bar was noisy and filled with professional people who thronged the bar. The noise was insane.

Jake found them a round table in a corner, a bit away from the bar. She hoisted herself up on a stool and picked up the paper menu tucked into a holder in the center of the table. She glanced through it as a waitress approached with a ready smile for Jake.

"Hi, Jake," the woman said. "The usual?"

He nodded. "Hi, Bonnie. Why are you waiting tables? You own this place."

"I have three people out sick."

Merry smiled at the woman. Jake was obviously a regular. The waitress turned to Merry. "And you?"

"Do you have Blackthorn Ale?"

"We sure do, honey," the woman said as she scribbled on her pad. "Our dinner special is shepherd's pie."

"And I'll have a shepherd's pie." Merry loved shepherd's pie. Her parents had taken her to England for her high school graduation gift. They'd spent days wandering the Cotswolds, peering into the bakeries, the smoky pubs and eating in the tiniest of restaurants. Merry's favorite was Sally Lunn's in Bath. She'd been back to Bath twice since then, and each trip had been special.

"Me, too," Jake said.

Bonnie smiled and walked back to the bar, calling in their order.

"She looks familiar," Merry said.

"She was big in the eighties. Had her own band, the Golden Octopus."

Merry knew that name. "My mother listens to them. That's why she looks familiar. Her photo is on all the albums."

"Which are still selling reasonably well."

"Is she your client?"

"For a while she was. Bonnie was one of the smart ones. Had her act together, kept her money and when travelling three hundred days a year got old, she bought this place. She now owns five of them throughout Southern California, as well as this whole block."

"So not everyone who comes to you needs your help."

"A few just want investment advice, which I'm happy to provide."

Bonnie returned with their drinks. Merry took a sip of the ale and smiled. "Perfect."

Bonnie smiled happily and said she'd be back with their food.

Merry cupped her chin in her hand and gazed at Jake. "When you heard I was coming to work for your dad, did you think I was one of the lost souls?"

"My sister thought you were a gold digger trying to use my dad to revamp your career. If she weren't so busy with the beginning of her new semester right now, she'd be dogging you every step of the way."

"Why would you think that? I don't understand why you would think working for your dad would revive my career. That doesn't make any sense."

"It wasn't so much my thought as my sister's. After a long conversation with her, I was able to persuade her to stay cool."

"What were your thoughts about me?"

"I'll admit I had my own concerns, which were why I stepped in to keep an eye on the money. But…" His voice trailed off as he studied her.

"Do tell me you've had a change of heart," she coaxed.

"I'm a little more open to what you're doing," he said.

Bonnie came back with their shepherd's pies and set the large bowls in front of them.

"That's a ringing endorsement," Merry said when Bonnie had left. She dipped her fork into the crusty potato topping, her mouth already watering.

"That's all I've got," he said, and took a long drink of his beer. "About the other night…"

"No big deal," she said, waving his words aside. Noelle had told her to act as if nothing happened. She moved uncomfortably on the stool.

"But I want to explain something." He paused, staring down at his food. "I liked *Maddie's Mad World*."

Merry drew back in surprise. "You're kidding me."

He shook his head. "It's true. Chloe was always so loyal to Maddie, and Maddie's adventures were fun."

"Chloe was boring," Merry said. "She was the eternal best friend who always knew how to get Maddie out of trouble."

"She wasn't boring," Jake replied.

"Don't get me wrong. I loved playing her, but she was the bright and cheerful daisy standing next to the elegant orchid."

"You're being too harsh on yourself. Chloe was smart and capable and she always had the right answer. No matter what madcap problem Maddie created, Chloe was always able to figure it out."

"She never got the guy. She had the weirdest clothes. She went through the entire six years of the series having a crush on this one guy who had no eyes for anyone but Maddie."

"So you would have had the character move on."

"Yes. I understand that real life, despite the prevalence of reality shows, just isn't that interesting. And the only people in fiction who get to be smart are detectives or scientists who have to figure out how to stop the zombie invasion."

"So you're saying that literature and movies and TV shows are populated by dumb people."

She nodded. "Dumb decisions make drama. Look at Captain Ahab. Did he really need to hunt that whale? I think not. And look how that turned out for him. And really, Anna Karenina, get on the train. It's not like the guy wasn't a drunk or a gambler. This doesn't make for the most stable of relationships. So why kill yourself over him? And why do so in such a gruesome manner? Take pills instead."

"Wow," he said with a broad smile.

"Don't get me wrong. I like reading about other people's stupidity. I understand stuff happens and people have to fight their way out of it, but a lot of times, people volunteer for the situation."

"Are you saying you've never made a dumb decision in your life?" he asked.

"I've made plenty. Luckily, none of them have been dumb enough to make the news or provide inspiration for a book, a movie or a TV show. Who knows, if Chloe had made some stupid decisions in her life, maybe she'd have been worthy of her own TV show."

"You don't seem to like Chloe."

"I loved her," Merry answered, "but she was still boring. I thought the show would be a springboard to a long career. But the one thing I learned was that I was just an accessory, sort of like a knockoff purse."

"I don't know what to say."

"I'm a realist. My parents are realists, which is why I never ended up as one of your clients. I may have been playing a TV character, but my feet were firmly planted in reality. That's one of the problems with a lot of actors. They keep playing make-believe after the cameras stop rolling."

Merry took another bite of her shepherd's pie. The savory sauce, the crispy crust of the potatoes and the tender chunks of beef were the best she'd ever eaten. "No one has ever asked me questions like this before. The only people I've ever discussed the show with were my family. The paparazzi were only interested in looking up my skirt. The entertainment shows just wanted me to act crazy. The producers wanted me to provide positive publicity. Maddie was whole bucket full of crazy for the network. Her behavior embarrassed everyone." She licked her fork and took a deep sip of her ale. "Do you know why the show ended, considering the great ratings we were getting?"

"Why did it end?"

"'Cause Maddie was nuts and she decided she didn't want to be on the show anymore. She wanted to concentrate on being a film actress, and the rest of us got left behind." And look how that had turned out. Now Maddie had nothing and couldn't get a part to save her life. Maddie's path of self-destruction had been so memorable no one would give her anything. Merry felt a little sad for Maddie.

She finished her ale and asked Bonnie for water when she returned to ask if Merry wanted a refill. The pub had gotten noisier and more crowded. A football game played on the TV behind the bar and shouts went up every few minutes over some play.

"I'm sorry," Jake said.

"Don't be sorry for me. I tried the movie and TV route, but Maddie's reputation tarnished me, as well. Maddie took her clothes off for *Playboy* every few years and ran around on reality shows, but I went in a different direction. I'm doing okay. I'll never be on *Hollywood Rehab*." *Playboy* had approached her, too, but she kept her clothes on, with a very strong no to their offers. "You survived or you didn't. And let's face it, if people didn't survive, you would be out of a job."

He half grinned at that. Merry could see that his food was gone and his beer glass was empty.

"Ready for another beer?" he asked.

"No. I'm a lightweight. More than one beer and I'll be too sleepy to walk. As much as I would love to, I have to get up in the morning and figure out how to repair the displays. I think I'll just go home and order shoes online. It's much safer."

"No night at the Mission Inn," he teased. He signaled Bonnie and she brought the bill, which he paid with his credit card.

He looked so cute when he teased her.

"Another time," she responded. She slid off the stool. "Thanks for the meal and the ale."

"I'll see you in the morning, then."

Bonnie brought the slip back; he signed it and then followed Merry out the door.

They stood on the street. The Mission Inn was ablaze with light. Built in an eclectic mixture of styles that had a definite Spanish look, the inn dominated the downtown area. It was a favorite place for her to go when she wanted to get away from life.

They walked silently to the parking garage. Merry wondered what had possessed her to go on a second date with him. If she succumbed to her desire, she'd be kissing him. She tensed, thinking about how his lips would feel on hers. In a moment of weakness, she'd let her guard down.

Merry touched the remote for her car and unlocked it. "Thank you for dinner. I appreciate your taking the time to let me relax and not think about the damage to the displays."

"It's fixable," he insisted yet again.

"Okay. Good night." She opened the door to her white Prius and gave him a cheerful wave. *Get out of here,* she chanted in her head. *Get as far away as possible before you really do give in to the desire to kiss him.*

As she drove away, heading for the freeway, she wondered how she was going to avoid him. He was too tempting, too desirable. He made her feel hot and cold at the same time. He made her want to be wild.

Jake was so different from the men she'd dated in the past. She'd tended to be attracted to men in the entertainment business who understood the stresses of the industry and the toll they could take on a person. She'd tended to stay away from high-powered men like Jake who were intense and competitive.

Her phone rang and she tapped the screen at the center of her car to answer it. "Hello, Mom."

"Hello, darling. I just had to call you. I'm so excited," Janet Alcott said.

Merry's mother designed stained glass windows. "What's exciting?"

"I've just been handed the job of designing five windows at St. Matthew's Church. They loved my preliminary sketches, and I needed to tell someone. Noelle isn't answering her phone and your dad is on his way to Paris. Then he has a twelve-hour layover, then on to Rome with another twelve-hour layover and back to LAX. I won't see him for three days."

"I'm happy for you," Merry said as she navigated the traffic on the freeway. "How are you going to celebrate?"

"Your father was planning on taking a couple weeks off, but I'm thinking I might hop the next plane to Rome and meet him. He needs a break. I emailed him, but I haven't gotten a reply yet."

Her father kept his iPad with him all the time, even in the cockpit of the jumbo jets he piloted. As soon as he had a break, he'd get back to her mother and then they'd be in Rome doing what the Romans excelled at.

"So tell me," her mother continued, "how is the amusement park going?"

Merry tried not to sigh. "Well, up until today's windstorm, I was ahead of schedule. Now I have a half dozen displays with enough damage to wreck my budget, but my boss's son is being less of a pain in the butt."

"Noelle told me all about him," Janet said with a chuckle.

"We just had dinner," Merry confessed.

"How did that go?"

Merry wasn't certain what to say. She generally didn't talk to her mother about her love life. Not that she'd had much of one before, but now all the possibilities with Jake left her reeling. "It was a pity dinner. He offered me food and drink to take my mind off the damaged displays."

"Sweetie," her mother said in a consoling tone, "you'll pick yourself up and do what needs to be done to get your displays back in order in plenty of time for your opening."

"I know. It's just hard," Merry said. All that work, only to have one afternoon of high winds put her back.

"You're not going to let a little setback like this get you down."

"Today I am," Merry said. Traffic slowed, and she realized she was seeing fire trucks parked on the side of the freeway. Powerful floodlights scanned a blackened area. She smelled smoke but didn't see any fire. The firemen must have already contained it and put it out. Just the threat of fire was enough to make her shudder. She sighed again.

"It is now 7:37 p.m., which means you have another four hours and twenty-three minutes to brood."

"I know, Mom. I just want to get home and indulge in some internet shoe buying to take my mind off my job for a couple hours."

"You'll be fine, Merry. You should take a look at the

Prada boot line. I'm really lusting after this one pair. And since I'll be in Rome, I think I'll check them out."

Merry grinned. No wonder her mother wanted to go to Rome. "Have fun."

"Do you want me to call you back at midnight to make sure you're not brooding anymore?"

"No, thank you. I'm really not going to make it to midnight. I need to be up early tomorrow."

"You get a good night's sleep. I'll call you from Rome when I get there."

"I'm so jealous," Merry said.

"I know, dear." Her mother disconnected.

Merry went back to concentrating on her driving.

Connor Bentley was the youngest mayor ever elected to office in Riverside. He was tall and slender with dark brown eyes and an easy smile. He was suave and sophisticated, and watching him smile at Merry made Jake furious. And he didn't know why.

John Walters shook hands with the mayor as Jake approached them.

"Connor," John said, "you remember my son, Jake."

Jake shook the mayor's hand. "What brings you all the way out here?"

"Just checking on the progress. I'm planning a family event for the city employees and I wanted to talk to John about hosting it." Connor glanced around. "I'm happy to see this old place get a new lease on life. It's a landmark here in Riverside."

Merry grinned at Connor. "I've heard about this community's attachment to the park."

"We're not the mouse house, but we do just fine," John said. "And I credit Merry here for her brilliant ideas and putting everything together the way she is."

"I can see that." Connor's gaze rested on Merry for a moment too long and Jake wanted to put his arm around her to let Connor know who the competition was.

Merry grinned. "Do you want a tour?"

"I sure do."

"We're still fixing the windstorm damage from last week, but everything is back where it belongs, and the displays are now firmly anchored to the ground."

John followed while Merry started to give an overview of what they had been doing. Jake found himself trailing along behind them. Merry talked in an animated manner as she explained about the retail area and what was going into the different stores.

As he watched them, Jake made a decision. He wasn't going to let this slick politico show him up. Merry opened the door to one of the retail stores, and her sister stepped out. As Merry introduced Connor to Noelle, Jake pulled his phone of his pocket and dialed Billy Johnson. Billy Johnson was an original member of the boy band The Brothers J. Billy and his brothers had been looking for the perfect venue to get back together. Jake suddenly knew they'd be perfect for the grand opening.

Connor and Noelle chatted and then he stepped into her store. Jake stood outside, waiting for Billy to answer his phone. Jake had been their financial manager for nearly five years.

Billy answered. "Jake, good to hear from you."

In the background Jake heard a dog barking and a baby crying. He explained about the grand opening and the park and what he needed. When he finished, Billy was silent for a moment. "Sounds good. I'm in. I'll get with my brothers and call you back in twenty."

Jake disconnected, keeping his sense of triumph under control. Connor was flirting with Noelle as he looked at her display cases. Noelle appeared completely immune to Connor's charm. She showed him her glassware and he seemed impressed.

"We're putting in a bakery, specializing in Russian baked goods, on the corner by the ticket booths," Merry explained.

"The scent of baked goods will entice every person who walks in," Connor said.

And encourage people to buy more. The wonderful scents of cinnamon, sugar and yeast culminating in the perfect bun always primed the pump, so to speak. "We have a number of merchants who've already signed on," John said, "but we still have four empty stores."

"I'll put the word out and see what I can find for you," Connor said in a cordial tone. He winked at Merry, who smiled back.

His phone rang and Jake answered it. "Billy, I thought you said twenty minutes."

"I didn't even have to pitch your idea. My bros are all for it."

Jake sighed in relief. "Not much in the way of pay."

"We'll work it out," Billy said. "The real money is in merchandise anyway."

"I'm sure we can arrange something," Jake responded. They talked a few more minutes, then Jake promised to get more info to Billy and disconnected.

He wanted to rush right over to announce The Brothers J would be performing at the park but hesitated, watching Merry show Connor an empty store still waiting for an occupant. He didn't like the way Connor seemed to hover over her or the way his hand brushed against her arm. He definitely didn't like the way Connor looked at her as though she were his for the taking.

Jake's father proudly showed Connor the display in

the center courtyard. A twenty-foot Christmas tree laden with large plastic ornaments in a rainbow of colors shared space with hundreds of plastic bows. Small plastic elves were hidden in it, peeking out from unexpected places. Merry was planning a contest for the children who visited the park on opening day. Find all the elves and receive a free visit next year. When lit, the tree could be seen from the road.

A movement caught the corner of his eye, and he glanced back to find Noelle standing in the doorway of her shop watching him, her eyes slightly narrowed, lips pursed and head tilted to one side.

"The mayor is really hot, isn't he?" she said in a low, purring voice, her gaze darting back and forth between Connor and Jake as though comparing them.

How was he supposed to respond to a statement like that? "Not my type." He turned toward her, noting the amusement in her eyes.

"He's definitely Merry's type." She watched Merry for a second, her eyes showing her love for her sister.

"Merry would never be taken in by that glitzy...uh, slick..." He couldn't finish the sentence without revealing how he was starting to feel about Merry. And that feeling was spiraling out of control. He was a man who liked control because he dealt with craziness every day. Women didn't make him crazy, but something about Merry had caught him and wouldn't let go. He liked his women to be professional. He tended toward lawyers, bankers and even a college professor who'd taught logic. They were all safe and, like him, kept control of their lives. Merry was too volatile, too...artsy. He had the feeling that as soon as the Christmas season was over, she'd be leveraging herself into another job, no matter how she protested that she enjoyed being right where she was.

Jake had always had a conflicting set of feelings for the park. He'd practically grown up here, but he didn't have the same passion as his father. He couldn't imagine anyone else feeling the same passion.

"You don't look happy," Noelle said. "And I can't seem to figure out why. The park is going well. Your clients are still crazy. What could be the problem?"

He shook his head. He finally got it. She was messing with his head. "You're a sly one, aren't you?"

She tilted her head up. "I have no idea what you mean."

He studied her. "What's your game?"

She looked thoughtful as she stepped back into the store. He followed her into the coolness. In the background, the air conditioner hummed slightly. A stack of boxes sat on the counter waiting to be opened. Several of the displays had already been filled with an assortment of animals. The sun streamed through the window and caught the clear glass animals flashing a rainbow of colors on the walls.

"I don't have any game." She picked up a bear figurine and held it up to catch the sun.

"I don't believe you. I know game and I know gamers." He had plenty of clients who played games with themselves, each other and the public that bought what they had to offer.

She replaced the clear glass bear on the display and stood in the center of the room, studying him. A cunning smile curled her lips. "You like my sister, don't you?"

"She's okay. She's nice." And kissable. Where had that thought come from?

"Look at you trying to play it all cool."

He didn't answer.

"Why haven't you asked her out on another date?"

"I don't think I'm her style." Their dates hadn't exactly been stellar moments in his life. Though he had enjoyed their dinner at the brewpub.

Noelle laughed. "I know what you think your style is."

"And that is?"

"You like women who don't burden you with their problems," she replied. She walked behind the counter and opened a box, her face thoughtful. "You probably date women who don't have a lot of time or make too many demands because they have so many burdens on their time." She held her finger to her chin. "Professional women like bankers. Probably lawyers, too. Women who are too busy developing their careers to put time into having a relationship. I understand, because you have a very stressful job."

"I like my job." He flushed at the accuracy of her description.

"I didn't say you didn't. I said you like women who don't burden you with wanting a relationship."

"You don't know me."

"Yes, I do. You're all about keeping your options open. I can understand you. I like keeping my options open, too."

Jake wasn't certain he liked the way the conversation was going. He didn't like being psychoanalyzed, especially by Noelle. He sort of liked her, but in a different way from her sister. Merry stirred his senses. Noelle was more like a kid sister.

"Noelle Alcott, you're all right." He turned and walked out the door into the hot afternoon sun, shading his eyes as he searched out Merry, who was still standing in the courtyard with the mayor hovering around her.

Chapter 8

Merry loved showing the mayor around the park. He said all the right things in all the right places as he admired each display and the way the water park had been turned into Santa's castle. A thrill of excitement coursed through her. Though they were a month away from opening, she could finally see things coming together.

"Miss Alcott," Connor said, "you have certainly turned this park into something I never thought I'd see."

"Worried I'd sell out to the developers, were you?" John asked.

Connor didn't respond for a second. Merry could tell he was probably weighing the taxes a new housing development and strip mall would generate compared to what the park brought in. While he formulated an answer, Jake walked up, the wind ruffling his hair. He had a smug, satisfied look on his face.

"I have news," Jake said.

Merry gave him a questioning look. "What?"

"Do you remember The Brothers J?"

She nodded. "Boy band in the early nineties. Great dance music. Totally hot."

"I've tentatively gotten them to agree to help launch the opening weekend."

Merry's mouth fell open. "You did?" Her brain rapidly went into planning mode. "Wow. How did you manage that?"

He shrugged. "Just a phone call."

She didn't have to rely on her own contacts after all. "Opening day is going to be awesome." She paused to think. "But before I get really excited, is this coming out of my budget?"

"No. We haven't worked out all the details, but you don't have to worry about your budget."

Connor started laughing. "I remember them. My older sister was crazy for that group. Had posters all over her bedroom. I'll have to let her know. She'll be here."

"Will you be with her?" Merry asked.

"Will you?"

She smiled happily. "Of course." She glanced at Jake to find him tightening his jaw. "Thank you, Jake. You've just made opening weekend the best."

"I aim to please."

"I am duly impressed." And that was one thing on her to-do list she didn't have to do.

Connor's cell phone rang, and he took it out of his pocket. "Sorry, I have to take this. I'll see you tonight at seven, Merry." He turned and walked away.

"I have to get back to work," John said. "Send me the particulars on the band and I'll get the info to the marketing department. They're going to have to work fast."

"You have a date with him?" Jake watched the mayor

head swiftly toward the parking lot, the phone still to his ear.

"He talked me into giving him a shot at letting us have a permanent historical display here in the park. It seems the historical museum on Market has lost its lease and the owners want to make into a retail store now that the downtown area is really starting to turn around."

"Does this include dinner?"

"I'm always up for a free meal," she retorted. "You're making all kinds of weird faces. What's up with that?"

His face stilled as she watched him, wondering why he suddenly seemed agitated.

"I'm not making weird faces," he objected.

"Okay, but your eye is twitching still." What was bothering him?

"He's a slick guy. You watch out for him."

Her eyebrows rose. "What do you mean?"

"You're on his agenda."

"You make it sound like he's all about seducing me."

"I went to high school with him. Trust me, he had all the girls dancing to his tune."

"Well, I'm not the kind of woman who is easily impressed. So stop worrying about me. This is just a business dinner."

"If it's just a business dinner, can I come?"

"No," Merry said. "I don't need a babysitter, though I do thank you for offering." She was just having a business meeting over dinner. Why would Jake react like this? As if he was jealous or something. He had nothing to be jealous about, since they had nothing going on between them. Men! She didn't need this crap. What she needed was to get back to work.

She stalked to her office without another word, her back stiff and her brain in a whirl.

She slammed the door to her office and went to sit in her chair, glaring at her computer. The cool hum of the air conditioner settled her nerves, though her thoughts wouldn't stop. What the hell was wrong with Jake? They'd gone out on exactly two dates in which nothing really happened except for an almost kiss. And now he acted as though she belonged to him. Where did she go from here?

She gripped a pencil and her notebook, idly doodling, her thoughts going in circles. Eventually she forced her thoughts into order and started thinking about the displays for the amphitheater to welcome The Brothers J.

Jake needed to get away. He climbed into his car and drove back to his Hollywood office. Even though he could work from anywhere, he liked his office and needed to put distance between him and Merry.

"I have a ton of things for you to go over and sign," Vicki said when he walked into his office. "All on your desk. Nothing serious."

"I'll take care of it."

"And call Judge Nichols. Right away," she said, her hand already on the phone.

Jake settled into his chair with a sigh. He liked being in his office. No sounds of hammering or wheelbarrows or construction people shouting at each other. Though the heat hadn't totally abated, downtown Hollywood was a lot cooler than Riverside.

His phone rang and he picked it up to hear Amy Nichols greet him.

"Good afternoon, Judge Nichols," he said.

"I have a bad one for you, Jake." Amy Nichols was a sixtysomething, four-foot-nine-inch spitfire.

"Tell me."

He heard papers rustling in the background and then she came back on the line again. "Cooper James."

"From the thrash-metal band Death Claw?"

"That's the one."

Jake had heard of him, from the infamous streaking incident on Wilshire Boulevard to the drug overdose and the drive off the end of Santa Monica pier, narrowly missing hundreds of tourists. "Why me?"

Amy took a long breath. "He's been in bankruptcy court three times in the past ten years. If anyone can help him and his six children—all by six different mothers, mind you—it's you. He's had two court-appointed conservators who couldn't control him, and I really didn't want to give him to you because I like you a lot. But his wife, with whom he has no children, wants you. She heard you're the best, and for some reason this woman still loves him. Though I can't understand why."

"Maybe she wants to make sure he's financially stable before she divorces him. That's what I would do."

Amy chuckled. "Me, too. I have to warn you, he's bad news. The last conservator ended up in the hospital."

"What happened?" This didn't sound good. Jake opened his laptop and started an internet search. His head was saying no, but his gut was saying this would be his Mount Everest. His reputation would be set for life if he could get this guy in decent financial shape.

"A bleeding ulcer," she said after a long pause. "There just aren't that many people I depend on."

"I'll meet with him and see how it goes. But I'm not making any promises."

"I wouldn't expect you to," Amy said. "I'm sending everything now."

"Thanks."

She disconnected. He spent a little more time researching Cooper James and allowed himself to be pulled into the challenge. He didn't have to think about the park, Merry or his father. He liked getting back to feeling normal, and deep down inside his accountant soul, he liked normal. He could function in normal.

For the next hour, he went through the files the judge sent him. Cooper James's finances were in a mess, more than a mess. There were so many tangles it was a wonder Cooper had any money at all. The more he dug into it, the more his palms itched to put everything to rights.

He liked having this kind of control. As much as he was attracted to Merry, he didn't like the way she did things. She always seemed to be flying by the seat of her pants. He understood that in her industry she had to work this way. She functioned well in chaos. He admired that in her. But working with numbers was different. B always followed A. Everything had its place and its logical conclusion. Everything had to add up.

He liked fixing people's financial woes. Merry didn't need fixing; she knew exactly what she was doing, how she was going to do it and what the final outcome would be despite the turmoil she frequently operated in.

Suddenly, the door to his office was flung open, and banged against the wall. Jake looked to up to find a man and woman stalking into his office. The woman was tall and graceful with artfully bleached blond hair, vibrant blue eyes and designer clothes. She looked to be in her late forties. She was slim and graceful looking, and would be pretty if not for the scowl on her face directed at her companion.

The man was tall and lean with tattoos covering both arms. Dark brown hair streaked with blond hung to his shoulders. He wore leather pants and a matching leather vest with a heavy gold chain. He slouched as though that made him look like a bad boy. He sat down in a chair un-asked and crossed one booted foot over his knee.

"Be polite, Cooper," the woman said angrily.

"I don't need somebody controlling my life. I have you."

"You will not have me for long if this behavior con-tinues."

A look of shock crossed his face and he hung his head.

This woman was done, Jake thought. Cooper James was about to meet his Waterloo.

"I'm Jake Walters," Jake said, standing with his hand out. The woman graciously accepted his handshake, but Cooper James ignored him. Jake gestured the woman to the other chair and she sat delicately on the edge.

"I'm Narissa James and this is my husband, Cooper." She gestured at the sullen man next to her.

Narissa had been a hot model in her day. She'd graced the covers of *Sports Illustrated, Vogue* and *Cosmo.* He couldn't help but wonder why she was with Cooper.

"I don't wanna be here," Cooper said.

"Fine," Narissa said. "You can wait outside."

"Gimme the car keys," he said with a pout.

"Wait outside," Narissa ordered in a stern tone that turned Cooper even more surly.

He lurched to his feet and left in an angry huff, slam-ming the door after him.

This woman didn't need a financial adviser, she needed a therapist.

"You wonder why I stay with him, don't you?"

How could he not? "You're a beautiful woman. You could go back to modeling."

"We have six beautiful children—Cooper and I. None of them are biologically mine. I get rid of him, they go, too. One of the nicest things I can say about him is that he had good taste in choosing his kids' mothers."

"I don't understand."

She reached over and patted his hand. "And that scares you, doesn't it?"

"How can a man have good taste in that?"

She stared at him thoughtfully. "I can't have children. Those babies were all a gift from Cooper for sticking it out and staying with him. After the children's mothers had them, I paid those women a lot of money to go away. What happened to them afterward, I had no control over. In two years, our eldest is going to be going to college. Chanel has wanted to go to Vassar since she was three years old and I'll be damned if that stupid, irresponsible, narcissistic, spoiled…"

Jake held his hand up to ward off the litany.

"Thank you for stopping me," she said with a sigh. "I could have gone on for another thirty minutes."

"Do you love him?" The question slipped out unintentionally. He hadn't meant to ask it.

"It's hard not to love a man who writes songs about you and gives you six of the most beautiful children ever. And none of them take after him, except for Sean. When he plays the violin it's like a glimpse into heaven. I didn't make the decision for me. Amber's mother is in prison. Kurt's mother overdosed. Where were these children going to go? They had no one but me. He loves those children and I know he loves me, but he's like a bee from flower to flower to flower." She stopped to take a deep breath.

"Okay, so this isn't about him, but you and those children. You and I will take care of the money. I can file the paperwork and put all the assets in your name."

"Can we do this without him?"

He studied her. "All you have to do is tell him where to sign. I don't think he'll turn you down. Then we'll put him on an allowance and start getting your finances back into order." Jake gave another look. "It's not as bad as it looks on paper."

"He feels if he's a rock star, he has to live like a rock star. I'm totally and completely overwhelmed. I used to be able to handle everything, but I don't have six children, I have eight. Cooper is two of them put together."

Jake sat back and found himself already formulating a plan of attack for her.

"For the first time in years, I feel as though I'm not spinning my wheels. Every financial planner, or wealth builder as the last one billed himself, I've dealt with in the past were just too caught up in the glamour of being next to a star. But you make me feel like you're my ally."

"I haven't been starstruck for a long time. Most of my clients end up in a better place. I get them out of their messes, teach them what to do and usually they're scared enough to stay on the right track. Some people I can't help. But you I can help. We both know you're running the ship. Narissa, you're going to be okay."

Relief flooded her face and for the time being the tension left her shoulders. "Thank you. Financial planner, therapist and savior all rolled into one."

"If you ever need a mechanic, let me know. I spent ten summers keeping my father's amusement park running."

"I'll keep that in mind."

"I have some forms you need to read over and sign. So let's get Cooper back in and get started."

After Narissa and Cooper James had left, Vicki came in with an envelope in her hand. "Have you decided on whether or not you're going to the Music Awards yet?"

She waved the envelope at him. "I need to have an answer today."

Jake sat back in his chair, thinking. A client, Victor Taylor, had given him the tickets, and he really needed to go to show support.

"I don't have a date."

"Then get one," Vicki said impatiently. "You've never had a problem getting a date before. You're nice, you have money, you don't smell bad and you have good manners."

"Thanks, I think." The problem wasn't getting a date but trying to figure how to ask Merry so she didn't turn him down. He didn't want to go with anyone else.

His cell phone rang and, seeing Merry's name on the display, he answered.

"Hi," she said. "I just wanted you to know that I hired the elves today, their costumes are fitted and I'm still underbudget."

"You enjoyed making this phone call to tell me that, didn't you?"

"Is that wrong of me?" she asked.

He heard the pride in her voice. Despite their rocky start, she'd managed to come in underbudget on every project except one. "No. You have every right be pleased."

"Are you pleased?"

The best opening. "How about as a 'yay team' incentive, I take you to the Music Awards in a few weeks?"

"You need a date, don't you?" Amusement colored her tone.

He almost squirmed. "One of my former clients gave me tickets. He always does, but I don't always go." His former client had been a musician before deciding he didn't want to tour anymore, and had turned to producing. He sent a lot of his troubled clients to Jake.

"It sounds like fun. I haven't been to one of those in a long time."

"And we've been invited to the after-party, too."

"That works for me."

Merry disconnected. For a moment, she was too stunned to move, and then she leaped out of her chair and ran out the door, racing to find her sister.

"Noelle," she half screamed as she barreled into her sister's shop.

Noelle stood on a ladder positioning some of her more expensive glass where little hands couldn't get to it. "What?"

"You'll never guess what just happened."

"I'm not good at guessing games, so just tell me."

"I'm going to the Music Awards with Jake."

Noelle looked up startled. "What?"

Merry hugged herself with so much excitement she almost fell over. "What am I going to wear? I don't have anything to wear."

Her sister jumped down from the ladder. "I know what you can wear."

Merry looked at her sister and they grinned at each other. "The dragon shoes. I've been dying to wear them. But I don't have anything to wear them with."

"They'll look fabulous. All by themselves."

"I can just see me naked in dragon shoes." Merry rubbed her forehead. "I don't think so."

"You've got the dragon dress. The Emilio Pucci. I'll call Betsy and she'll do something fabulous with your hair. You'll look awesome. You do remember how to put on mascara, right?"

"I know how to put on mascara."

Noelle stared critically at her. "Betsy will do your

makeup, too. And once you're there, you need to find Drake and throw yourself at him, get him all over my dress."

"Wow, you're a freak."

"Give me a moment. I'll feel ashamed about it later."

"I only let you talk to me like this because you're my sister and I love you."

Noelle waved her hand. "Whatever."

"I have to call Mom," Merry said, searching for her cell phone and realizing she'd left it in her office. Then she paused. "Why am I so excited about this?"

Noelle started laughing. "Maybe because a really hot man asked you on a really cool date. How long has it been since that happened?"

"You are so not amusing," Merry said with a sigh.

"I call them like I see them," Noelle said, once she'd stopped laughing. "Oh, look, here's Fenya. Did you bring any more of your baklava? We have to celebrate."

Fenya was a young woman with light brown hair and a sweet, round face. As the owner of the new Russian bakery across the courtyard, she'd started bringing some of her favorite pastries for the crew to try. "What are we celebrating?"

"My sister here has a really hot date."

"Pirozhki it is," Fenya said, turning around and heading back out the door. "I'll be back in a minute."

Noelle walked around her sister. "Can you take a week off to go to a spa? We have some work to do."

"Of course not," Merry replied, though the idea had merit. She hadn't had a spa date in a long time, and looking rested and pampered for her date always made her feel as if she could knock them all dead. She had work to do, and she was waiting for a shipment of lights to finish Santa's palace.

"I should get back to work." If she could. She hadn't been so excited in a long time. As she walked out into the afternoon heat, her sister started humming.

Chapter 9

Merry didn't get her week-long spa date, but she did get two days off to get ready for the awards ceremony. She spent the first day getting pampered at a spa. She was going to be with some of the most beautiful people in the music industry. If she was going to be recognized, she was going to look her best. Appearance was everything in entertainment. She would be competing with younger and prettier stars.

"You're perfect," Noelle said after her friend had finished Merry's hair and makeup.

Merry glanced at her jewel-encrusted watch. She had ten minutes until Jake showed up. She wiped her damp palms on a towel. She stood, and Noelle slid the dragon dress over her head. The silk folds flowed down to midthigh. The dress itself was a simple black sheath with a sinuous dragon curling down one side, the tail around her shoulder while the head lay just at the hem.

She stepped into the dragon shoes, a matching black silk with a dragon embroidered on the outside of each shoe, and studied herself in the mirror.

Betsy had pulled her hair back into a simple French twist. The makeup highlighted her large eyes and her brows. Her lipstick matched the red on her shoes and dress. The dress was just loose enough to swirl seductively, but still shaped enough to show her curves. *Jake Walters, eat your heart out.*

"I don't look like myself," she said to her image in the mirror.

"You look better than yourself," Noelle said as she draped a gold cuff bracelet over one wrist and inserted simple gold earrings in Merry's ears. "And this dress doesn't need any other adornment than this cuff and the earrings."

Merry dabbed a bit of perfume on the back of her hands and behind each ear. Her favorite perfume, Opium, went perfectly with the dress.

The doorbell rang and Noelle jumped. "He's here."

"He's early," Merry said.

She hurried to the door and opened it. Jake stood in the doorway looking so handsome in his tuxedo that her breath caught in her throat. His eyes widened at the sight of her.

"Wow! I should have brought flowers," he said, his gaze sweeping over her, admiration in his eyes.

"This isn't prom night. Though I did miss mine."

"Why did you miss your prom?"

"I was working on a movie in Mexico. One of those straight-to-video ones."

"You look fabulous," he said.

"Thank you," she said, grateful that she wasn't going to embarrass him. She hadn't been to one of these events in a very long time. She did get invited to a number of awards ceremonies and film festivals, but she usually gave her tickets to her mother or sister.

"Ready?"

She nodded. She was as ready as she'd ever be. He held out his arm and she tucked her hand around his elbow. She grabbed her red-and-gold clutch purse from the hall table and stepped out into the warm afternoon.

The limo was long and elegant, and once inside, he offered her champagne. She declined. This dress was not the kind to spill her drink on. The limo pulled smoothly away from the curb, and Merry glanced back to find her sister and her friend peering at her from the living room windows.

"You look nervous," Jake said.

"It's been a very long time since I've been to such a highly visible event." Awards ceremonies had always made her nervous. She'd once been a presenter at one and worried all the way to the podium that she'd trip over her dress or walk out of her shoes or say the wrong thing. She had those same nervous worries now, though her dress was short, she wasn't presenting anything and she wouldn't have to talk to anyone since she could let him do the talking.

"You don't have to worry about anything. We'll just have fun and enjoy the evening. So relax."

That was true. Who would remember who she was?

The drive was quick. Before Merry was even aware they'd arrived, the limo pulled smoothly into the long line of cars releasing people.

When their limo arrived at the red carpet, Jake got out and turned to hold out his hand. She wrapped her fingers around his, surprised at their warmth. She heard the click of cameras, newspeople trying to get a photo before they knew she wasn't anyone, as she put one foot on the curb and tried to exit the limo as gracefully as possible.

She stood and Jake smiled at her. A couple of photographers turned away, disappointed she wasn't someone, but a couple of photographers didn't. They snapped photos of her as she moved gracefully along, her hand curled around Jake's arm.

"Meredith Alcott," came a voice.

Merry turned her head.

"Meredith Alcott, is that really you?" A reporter at the side of the carpet waved at her. Merry smiled and walked over.

"Joanna Loza," Merry said. "I haven't seen you in years."

Joanna Loza was the entertainment reporter for a TV newsmagazine. She was small and slim, wearing a flame-colored, floor-length gown as beautiful as any in the line of celebrities making their way to the entrance to the theater. Her long blond hair curled around her shoulders and a necklace decorated with diamonds sparkled at her throat.

"You look beautiful," Joanna gushed holding up her microphone. "Who are you wearing?"

"Emilio Pucci dress with Louboutin shoes and purse," Merry answered automatically.

"We haven't seen you in forever," Joanna continued to gush. "What have you been up to?"

"Set designing now."

"We miss you in front of the camera," Joanna said.

"Thank you. It's nice to be missed."

"In this dress, sweetie, I don't think you'll be missed for too much longer. Are you staging a comeback?"

"Thank you for that." She felt Jake press a hand against her back and she walked away. She heard her name floating down the line and a few people turned to look at her. Suddenly, she wasn't nervous anymore.

Jake couldn't take his eyes off her. She was so beautiful; he couldn't believe she was with him. The scent of her perfume sent his pulse into overdrive. And that dress was perfect on her. No one else could have carried off this Oriental look.

"So," he said, "are you staging a comeback?" He guided her down the carpet. Someone waved at her and she smiled back.

She slanted an irritated glance at him. "Not on your life."

"Merry Alcott," came another voice. "As I live and breathe. Is that you?"

Merry turned to the woman approaching her. "Nora Kennedy."

Jake was impressed. Nora Kennedy was one of the most influential power brokers in the music business. She had started in TV the same time as Merry, but instead of continuing to act, she had turned to music and now not only had a successful singing career but had started to produce music videos for up-and-coming new talent.

Nora floated up to Merry. Her silver floor-length gown was a bit fussy for Jake's taste, but what did he know about gowns? He found himself comparing her to Merry's sophisticated look. In fact, he found himself comparing Merry to all the women standing around and chatting with reporters or posing for photos, and they all came off as second best.

"How have you been?" Nora asked after embracing and air-kissing Merry.

"I'm doing well. And you?"

"I'm doing terrific. I hear you're doing set design," Nora said.

"I am, and you're producing music videos."

Nora nodded. "I'm shooting my next one in March. Maybe we could work together. I could use your talents."

"That sounds like fun. Definitely contact my agent."

Jake was not sure he liked the idea of Merry moving on with her life. He knew it would happen; maybe he shouldn't have brought her to this event. He liked having her around the park with her challenging manner and in-his-face arguments.

Nora grinned. "And now that we don't have Mad Maddie in our lives anymore, we can have some real fun."

"That would be nice."

Nora waltzed away to greet someone else.

"Are you going to take the job?"

"I might. I like Nora. I think we could have been good friends except for Maddie. It could be fun to have that chance again. Though it depends on your dad."

Jake realized he was a little bit jealous. He'd brought her as his date and she was really working the room. He hadn't expected this. He dealt with the unexpected all the time, but here it was different. She wasn't leaping at the opportunity like some of his other clients would have. And he dealt with a lot of people who would go to the opening of an envelope, just to have the rush again. Merry was a levelheaded woman. Deep down inside, he was still surprised at her common sense.

"Jake Walters," Victor Taylor said.

"Vic," Jake replied, pleased to be recognized. Victor Taylor was one of the trashiest rappers on the planet, but God had paid him back by giving him three daughters, and he refused to let them listen to his music. His eldest was standing next to him, looking chic for all of her fifteen years. Vic was thin and muscular. He wore a black tuxedo with a plaid vest and white Nike running shoes. His daughter was dressed in a pretty floral gown that emphasized her youthfulness.

"I didn't think you'd come," Vic said. "I send you tickets every year." He smiled. "Or are you just trying to impress this beautiful lady?" Vic studied Merry. "I know you from somewhere."

"I'm Merry Alcott," she said, holding out her hand.

Vic frowned. "Something Margaret, no, Margie..." His voice trailed off.

"Maddie's Mad World," Vic's daughter supplied. "I watched your show. I love it so much." She bounced a little.

Jake found Vic giving him an appraising look. "How do you guys know each other?"

"She's doing some set designing at my dad's amusement park."

"Set designing," Vic said, his eyebrow going up. "I could use you. The last set designer for my video went overbudget, didn't know a curtain from a pillowcase and had no sense of color. How's your sense of color?"

"I have a sense of color and I can keep you underbudget." She nudged Jake, her eyes darting from him to Vic.

"And I can attest to that," Jake said, getting the hint.

"If Jake says you can stay underbudget, then I know it's true. I'll have my people contact your people." Vic wandered off to greet someone else. His daughter waved at Merry and she waved back with a smile.

"You've turned out to be the belle of the ball," Jake said, trying to keep his tone light and friendly, even though he wasn't feeling light and friendly.

"Are you upset?"

"No," he replied. "Just surprised. A lot of business is

done at these events, and I have no objection to you getting some business."

"I have not solicited any business," she said, her voice stiff.

"That's not what I mean." He wasn't certain he knew what he meant. Seeing her talk so smoothly with the movers and shakers in music had given him a new insight into who she was.

He heard a squeal and turned around to find Annie Gray walking toward him, dragging her own date. "Jake," she said, tottering toward him. She wore a pink mesh dress, and her panties and bra were clearly visible. Her hair was bleached blond with matching pink streaks. Even her lipstick matched. She was, well, pink.

"You're out of jail," Jake said, keeping his tone neutral.

"No thanks to you," Annie said, her gaze drifting over to Merry. "I see you went old school for a date. If I'd known you were attending, you could have brought me."

The last thing he would have wanted was to be seen as her date. "This is Merry Alcott. Merry, this is Annie Gray."

"You're one of his clients, too?" Annie asked.

"No, just a friend."

"Emilio Pucci," Annie said, gazing at Merry's dress. "I wanted that dress, but I had to settle for this old thing."

"I saved my pennies," Merry said with a sweet smile, the look in her eyes telling Jake just what she thought of Annie's "old thing."

Jake tried not to laugh as he compared Merry's cool elegance to Annie's mesh lamppost wear.

"Merry Alcott." A man pushed past Annie and grabbed Merry in a hug. "I haven't seen you for years. You grew up and you look awesome."

Merry dimpled at the man. Jake frowned, trying to

place the man. Then he remembered. Daryl Wicks. One of the best rappers in the business and very much in demand. Annie's eyes grew wide, and she tried to insinuate herself between Merry and Daryl.

"Daryl," Merry said with a laugh. "You grew up pretty good, too."

Daryl Wicks smiled at Jake. "Can you tell I'm one of Merry's cast offs?"

Merry playfully punched him in the arm. "Stop that. We had three dates."

"I know, and your guy needs to know that there is life after Merry."

Merry laughed again. "You make me sound terrible."

Jake just wanted to pull her away from him. And then something else clicked. "'Life After Merry,'" he said. "You wrote that song." He stared at Merry. "That song was about you?"

"My first number-one hit on the charts," Daryl said. "And I owe it all to Merry breaking my heart."

"I didn't break your heart."

"Mr. Wicks," Annie said, trying to get his attention.

"For the sake of music legend, yes, you did," Daryl said, ignoring Annie.

"Daryl," Merry said. "This is Jake Walters. I'm his date for the evening."

Daryl held out a hand. "Jake Walters. I've heard of you. You're a financial rock star."

"Thank you." Jake was surprised. He didn't think anyone at the pinnacle of success like Daryl would know about him. Normally the people who knew about him needed him. Daryl didn't need him.

"Mr. Wicks." Annie put a hand on his wrist and pouted as prettily as she could. She jiggled her breasts. But Daryl had no eyes for anyone but Merry.

"I sing," Annie said. "I'd love to work with you."

Daryl gave Annie a look that said he didn't recognize her, didn't know her and didn't want to know her. Annie looked stunned, and for a second the lost little girl deep inside came out, and she looked as though she wanted to cry.

Merry took one look at her. "Annie Gray, I want you to meet Daryl Wicks. Daryl, Annie is one of Jake's clients."

One eyebrow rose. "I thought you were out of the business, Miss Gray."

Her exploits were front-page material; the industry was still a small world and everyone either knew everyone or knew of them. Jake wasn't surprised that Daryl knew her history.

"No, no I'm not," Annie said in a rush. She glanced at Jake, biting her lips nervously. "I'm revamping my image."

Daryl studied her thoughtfully. "Let's get together sometime next week and we'll talk."

Annie looked ecstatic. "Yes, thank you." She drifted away as though she were walking on a cloud.

"She has talent, but terrible choice in material. I can help her," Daryl said. "If she ever decides she wants to be a singer and not just a pop star."

Jake didn't know what to say. This business was cutthroat, and this man had just been kind to a young woman with the personality of a child.

Merry leaned into him and kissed him on the cheek. "You always were one of the nicest guys in the business."

Daryl shrugged. "I learned a lot from you."

"In three dates," Merry said.

He leaned over. "It would have been more if I hadn't been such a jackass." He kissed her on the cheek. "I have to get ready for my opening number. I'll see you inside. If you ever feel like reliving the past..." He walked off.

"Are you going to call him?" Jake asked.

"That's not my life anymore, and believe it or not, I'm good with that."

Jake said nothing. They managed to get into the foyer, away from the hounding of the entertainment reporters and the photographers.

"You're an odd woman, Meredith Alcott."

Her eyebrows rose. "How so?"

"I've never met anyone in the business who graciously retired the way you have."

"It took me a while to be graciously retired," she replied.

An usher approached and Jake pulled the tickets out of his pocket and handed them to the young man. He led them into the theater and showed them their places.

Merry settled in her seat. She felt a little odd over all the attention she was receiving. Who knew she'd had that kind of impact? She'd once run into a couple of young teens who'd told her that her character had influenced their lives. She would never have thought that Chloe was so influential. To Merry she was just the girl who had cleaned up Maddie's messes.

And now being here at the Music Awards set her heart to pounding. So many people remembered her, and she was totally surprised.

"Are you all right?" Jake asked.

"Yes. Today was a little more eye-opening than I had expected."

"You thought you'd come here, blend in and no one would remember who you are."

"Pretty much," she replied.

"How does that make you feel?"

"No. We're not playing shrink today. Let's just enjoy the show." She settled back in her seat and took several deep breaths, trying to calm her jumping nerves.

Her mind leaped to the two offers for set design. She wasn't about to put that money into the shoe fund just quite yet. She needed to see if the offers were genuine or just people being polite. Though the prospect of working for them was exciting.

The seats were filling up fast. A discreet glance at Jake's watch told her the show would be starting in less then ten minutes. She was going to enjoy her evening with Jake and not think about anything else.

During the after-party, the ballroom was alive with music, flashing lights, the clink of china and glasses and a hundred people on the dance floor gyrating to the loud music. Waitstaff moved between tables, balancing trays and flutes of champagne and other drinks.

The beautiful people of the music industry were all having a great time, especially Merry. Jake sat at his table, hardly able to take his eyes off her. In her dragon dress, as she called it, she looked almost demure compared to the other women who in various states of revealing décolletage seemed overblown.

Merry's long-sleeved gown covered her from neck to midthigh without revealing a piece of skin other than her long legs. And yet she was the sexiest woman at the party. Merry didn't need to show skin to be sexy. Her self-confidence showed in the classy look of her dress and the matching shoes. The other women in the room, no matter how wealthy or famous, didn't even begin to compare to her.

Daryl and Merry were on the crowded dance floor and

Jake could barely contain the spurt of jealousy he felt. They looked good together, with their easy camaraderie and graceful moves. Merry was laughing and looked as though she was thoroughly enjoying herself.

Victor Taylor slid into the empty chair next to Jake. "You haven't taken your eyes off her for hours."

"She is my date," Jake said.

"How many years have we known each other?" Vic took a sip of his champagne. "I've met some of the women you've dated. And trust me. She's more than just a date."

Merry twirled around, the hem of her dress flaring and showing more of her beautiful legs. She tilted her head back and closed her eyes, her body swaying with the music.

Jake thought about that for a moment. "When I first met her, I was so prepared to dislike her that finding out she's not some psycho ex-celebrity trying to get back into the public eye has thrown me off my stride."

"Maybe somebody has become a tad too jaded about their profession."

Jake twisted to look at his friend. "What are you saying?"

Vic glanced thoughtfully at Merry and then back to Jake. "As long as I've known you, you've always stuck to really safe women. Women like you, committed to their career and, well…dull."

"Are you saying I'm dull?"

"I'm saying you think you like dull. And Merry isn't dull."

"No, since I've known her, my life has been sort of like being on one of my dad's roller coasters."

"You told me once you didn't like roller coasters." Vic took an olive from the table's vegetable centerpiece. "Have you changed your mind?"

The music had changed to a waltz and Daryl's hands seemed to be all over Merry except where they should be.

"Maybe," Jake finally answered.

"Then you need to get her away from Daryl. That man still uses women like hankies. Go dance with her, bro." Vic shoved Jake out of his chair.

Jake stepped through the dancers until he reached Daryl. He tapped Daryl on the shoulder and when the man looked up, Jake smiled and said, "My turn."

Merry smiled at him and walked into his arms, her body pressed against his as he led her into the first step of the waltz and whirled her around.

"Are you thinking about dating him again?" Jake asked with a tilt of his head at Daryl Wicks, who'd already found another partner.

"No," Merry said. "He's hard on the women he dates. And frankly, he just wants to date me so he can dump me."

"That's a little cynical," Jake said.

"You're probably right. Daryl hasn't found the right woman yet, and I know I'm not her."

She leaned her cheek against his shoulder, and he reveled in the sensation of her lean body against his. He could stay this way all night. The feel of her in his arms was so right, so…perfect. He wanted the dance to go on forever. He wanted to do more than just dance. He wanted more than a kiss, more than a moment of having her in his arms. He wanted to make love to her, to feel her beneath him in the throes of passion.

Jake was so startled at the trajectory of his thoughts, he almost stopped dancing.

"Let's get out of here," he said.

She let him lead her back to the table. She grabbed

her purse, and with her hand tightly in his, he led her out of the ballroom, through the hotel foyer and out into the cool November night.

Chapter 10

Merry couldn't believe she'd asked him in for a night-cap. She'd been even more surprised when he'd accepted. He'd dismissed the limo, saying he'd get a cab home, and now Jake sat in her living room, his tuxedo jacket neatly folded over the arm of the sofa and a glass of wine in his hand. She'd removed her shoes and neatly tucked them in a corner. She knelt in front of the fireplace and started a fire. She sat down on the fuzzy rug she kept there, and he joined her.

The fire flickered across his face. Something in his dark eyes sent her pulse racing and her heart pounding until she was breathless.

He wasn't taking a cab home. He was spending the night. And the thought of what was about to happen made her knees weak and her palms hot.

"I like your house," he said, looking around. "You have excellent taste in art."

"It's all mine," she replied. "I started drawing when I was barely out of diapers and as I grew older, I took a drawing pad and pencils with me everywhere I went. I have boxes of drawings in the attic." When she'd bought her house, she'd delved deeply into the arts and crafts period and at first created artworks to fit it. Then she'd fallen in love with Erté, and even though his art was classified as art deco, she loved the contrast between his lithographs and her furniture. Her own art began to reflect her love of his style.

His eyebrows went up. He tilted his head and half closed his eyes as he studied each canvas.

"I have more in the bedroom."

"I want to see them…eventually." He grinned at her.

She wanted to tease, to tantalize him. She ached to touch his skin, to run her fingers over the curve of each muscle.

"Thank you for this evening." The warmth of his knee pressed against hers. Heat exploded through her, spiraling down her spine in a burst of passion that made her gasp. "I enjoyed myself very much."

He set his wine down on a nearby table and then took her hand. "For a moment, I thought I was going to lose you to the media." He brought her fingers to his mouth and kissed the tips.

"Not a chance." Her skin tingled. She almost snatched her hand back at the flare of desire that touching him roused in her. "Have you finally decided I'm not going to hurt your father?"

"I've decided I want to kiss you." He slid his arms around her and pulled her to him. He leaned against a chair flanking the fireplace and gathered her close to him. She closed her eyes, taking in the feel of his body next to hers, his fingers on her skin.

Goosebumps rose on her arms. Her breath caught in her throat. His lips were warm and soft against her; his breath fanned across her cheek. She breathed deeply of his scent, like a forest after a rain.

A fire started deep in her stomach, radiating outward. She gasped at the strength of her passion, of her desire to grab him and tear off his clothes.

His fingers trailed gently down her neck to the swell of her breasts beneath the soft fabric of her dress.

He parted her lips, his tongue sliding against hers, his breath sweet. Heat flooded her.

"You are so soft." He nipped her ear, his tongue twirling around the lobe.

She shivered. Her breasts grew tight against her dress and heat curled its way across her skin. Her fingers started unbuttoning his shirt. She'd watched a TV show where the heroine seduced the hero by tearing his shirt off. Merry called it naked-chest seduction. The wild, uninhibited part of her wanted to tear Jake's shirt off, but the practical part of her said he'd have nothing to wear home later. She almost giggled at the oddness of her thoughts.

"And you are—" she ran her hand over his warm chest "—smooth." She flicked a nipple and it grew taut.

He kissed her again, so deeply she felt it all the way to her toes. She felt so alive, so in need.

He slid his hands down to the hem of her dress and slowly inched it up her legs exposing her black silk panties. She leaned away to allow him to remove it completely. He folded the dress carefully, as though preserving it for the distant future. He draped it over the arm of the chair.

"I like black lace," he said, sliding his fingers under her bra and testing the hooks.

She'd file that away for later. She pushed the sides of his shirt away and rested her head against him. She could hear the wild beat of his heart, matching the crazy thump of her own.

She couldn't remember how, but soon they were both naked and lying in front of the fire, curled up on the rug. His erection was rigid against her hip, his fingers swirling around her nipples and brushing against the undersides of her breasts, which had grown heavy and full. He slid down her body to kiss each nipple.

A flame of desire so intense grew from her core, and she cried out as his finger slid between the folds of her sex. *Oh, God. Oh, God,* she thought, panting with need and the passion of her growing orgasm.

"Protection?" she asked. She should have asked earlier.

"Taken care of." Then, gently, he parted her knees and slid between them, the hardness of his erection nudging against her core, and began to enter. Waves of pleasure crested as her muscles contracted around him. Tears gathered in the corners of her eyes. She threw her head back as he shuddered inside her. His body went rigid and hers seemed to shatter into a multitude of orgasms.

Jake couldn't believe he was finally where he wanted to be—in Merry's arms, touching the delicate perfection of her body. This exquisitely beautiful woman was finally his.

Having her on his arm at the awards show, surrounded by the most beautiful people in the world, had left him feeling as though he were walking on a cloud. The fact that she knew so many people and they remembered her with fondness had filled him with pride. She had chosen to be with him, and she was with him now. He had no doubt she could have had her pick of any number of men tonight. He had seen them watching her. One man had even murmured to Jake that he'd had a crush on Merry since he'd first seen her. Jake had been surprised. Somehow he had thought that his own crush on her had been unique, and to find out others had felt the same way surprised him.

Merry stirred in his arms. Her soft flesh hot against his brought him back to the present. He pressed a kiss on her brow. Heat rose inside him as he ran his hand down the side of her chest and up under the swell of her breast.

"Hmm," she said. "That was amazing."

Amazing wasn't the word he would have used. Incredible. Miraculous. He felt himself growing hard again. He didn't know what was going to happen tomorrow, but he knew right now what would happen next. As much as he enjoyed the comfortable, fluffy rug and the fire, he really wanted to be somewhere a little more conducive to making proper love to her.

She pushed away from him and stood, holding out her hands. "Come on. I love the fire and this rug as much as anything, but I know a place where we can be a lot more comfortable."

"You were reading my mind."

"Definitely." A mischievous twinkle showed in her brown eyes.

He let her draw him to his feet and followed her into the bedroom.

Merry sat in a lawn chair, her legs tucked up under her, a cup of coffee cradled in her hands. She wore white capri pants and a blue silk top with little white Ferragamo sandals she'd found at one of the designer outlet stores in Cabazon last summer. Noelle sat across from her, her laptop open. She tapped away, the keys making little clicking sounds as Noelle typed.

Noelle was dressed in a forest-green silk pantsuit with a cream silk blouse. A briefcase lay on the concrete next to her. She looked very professional with her black hair pulled back from her face in a sleek bob. She wore diamond earrings and an elegant glass hummingbird pin from her jewelry line on one lapel. She had only stopped in on her way to the airport before a flight to San Francisco to get the gossip and a bit of breakfast. Fortunately, Jake had just left.

The late-morning sun slanted across the pool and the water sparkled. A hot, dusty breeze rustled the leaves overhead. A squirrel sat on a branch watching them, tilting its head back and forth as though trying to decide if they were dangerous or not.

Behind the lattice fence, obscured by the thick wisteria, Merry could hear her neighbor's children laughing and talking as they played in their pool. Though it was the first week of November and the days were cooling off, it was still warm enough to swim if the pool was heated. The kids next door were enjoying their last moment of heat before the winter cold settled in across the Los Angeles basin.

"Two fires," Noelle said with a frown. "Just when I thought we'd get through fire season without any."

Merry said nothing as she sipped her coffee, thinking about Jake and wondering what was going to happen next with him.

"And here you are," Noelle cried. "Look who made the Who Worked the Red Carpet list." She turned the laptop toward Merry.

Merry saw herself posed against the backdrop of other celebrities. She looked a little uncomfortable with Jake's arm around her. The camera was pointed at her, and only a bit of Jake's chin could be seen to one side.

She leaned forward to read the caption. *Meredith Alcott, long missing from the red carpet, put in a special appearance last night at the Music Awards. She wowed the crowd in a hot little Emilio Pucci number and reminded us of how much we've missed her. Her shoes were Louboutin and perfectly matched to her dress. We're definitely hoping to see more of Merry Alcott.*

"That's nice," Merry said, her voice flat, wondering if Maddie was looking at the same photo. Maddie hated being eclipsed.

"Nice. Only nice," Noelle said. "Sweetie, nice is for puppies. You look fabulous. Do this right, you could have a career again."

Merry didn't think she wanted that. Last night had been marvelous and fun. But behind all the glamour, she could hear the backbiting, the competition, the anger, the snark and the sniping.

The constant need to look young, to be on the edge, was a lot of work, and she didn't want that for herself anymore. She didn't want to think about losing a role to some twenty-year-old who was cuter, with perkier breasts, a firmer butt and was willing to do what she needed to get where she wanted. Merry was done with that life. She'd had a good run and enjoyed the journey, but her life was so much more sane now. Maddie had always told her she was too nice. Merry always preferred nice over snarky.

"I like what I have. You know how I feel about crazy. Seven years with Maddie was crazy enough."

"I'm just testing you," Noelle said with a sigh. She sipped her coffee, then finished her croissant. "I don't want you back in that life, either. But my spidey senses

are telling me that something else happened last night."
She tilted her head, her expression amused.

Merry closed her eyes, the image of Jake kissing every
part of her body sending a thrill of desire through her. "I
slept with him last night."

Noelle's coffee cup dropped to the table to clatter on
the glass. "You...what?" She grabbed a pile of napkins
to mop up the spilled coffee. Fortunately, the cup hadn't
broken.

"I had sex with Jake last night," Merry repeated, feeling a hot blush creep up her cheeks. Every nerve in her
body relived the memory of his hot kisses, his warm body
against hers, his hands stroking her skin and... She covered her face with her hand.

"You had sex with him last night! Wow!" Noelle held
up her hand. "Way to end the dry spell, big sis."

"Really?" Merry said. "Is that all you can say?"

Noelle giggled. "How do you feel about it?"

Merry stared down into the dark brown depths of her
cup. She wasn't certain what she wanted to tell her sister.
"My eyes still haven't unrolled yet."

"Wow!" her sister repeated. "What are you going to
do?"

"We're two grown people. We had sex. We didn't sign
a Middle Eastern peace treaty."

Noelle giggled again. "Are you going to see each other
again?"

"That's a stupid question, Noelle. We work together."

"You know what I mean." Noelle refilled her cup from
the carafe on the table and lounged back in her chair. She
lifted her face to the late-morning sun and closed her
eyes. "How did he feel about it?"

"I'm thinking the man had no complaints." Merry
lowered her head so her sister couldn't see her face or

the way her cheeks burned. The memory of Jake Walters in her bed still filled her with excitement. Wonderful didn't even begin to describe what had happened. "I don't how to play it. Should I be cool like nothing happened? Lovey-dovey? Nonchalant? I don't know."

"You seem to be having a little bit of a conundrum here," Noelle said. Merry had given her sister a new word-a-day calendar once and one of the words had been conundrum, which had become Noelle's favorite word.

"I don't like having those," Merry admitted. She took a bite of her croissant and chewed it thoroughly.

"What happened this morning?"

"He fed my cat and made me breakfast."

"Oh, there's a double entendre there, but I'm not going to touch it," Noelle said with a half laugh.

"Then he called a cab and left."

"Was breakfast awkward?" Noelle leaned forward.

"Kind of. But not the way you're thinking." The awkwardness had been more on her side than his. He'd acted as though he woke up at her house every day of the week. And the way he'd made himself at home in her kitchen had startled her. She'd never dated a man before who liked to cook, even though he wasn't very good at it.

Noelle shook her head. "So how was it awkward?"

"He's not that great a cook." Merry tried not to think about the eggs on her plate with a lump of unmelted cheese in the center and the too-crisp bacon. Jake's enthusiasm, and the way he'd used more pans than he needed, had made up for the soggy mess on her plate, which she'd eventually hidden beneath her napkin.

"So you had to fake it, huh?"

"Seriously," Merry said. "But then again, maybe he was just nervous, too."

"Are you going to talk to him about his little problem?"

"Other than at work, I don't know if we're going to… see each other again."

"Now that we've gotten that out of the way," Noelle said, "who did you see last night and who was a train wreck?"

"I ran into Daryl Wicks."

"Seriously?" Noelle perked up.

"Yes."

"How did it feel to come face-to-face with your teenage rebellion?" She grinned merrily.

"He's grown up. A little bit. Kinda." She'd enjoyed seeing Daryl, even though he had been, as her sister said, her "teenage rebellion."

"Sleeping with Jake aside, were there any sparks between you and Daryl?"

"Not on my end. His end, I don't give a crap."

"He was a bucket full of crazy," Noelle said. She poured more coffee into her cup from the carafe.

"If I'd known then what I found out later, I would never have dated him." Even if it had only been three dates. She'd barely escaped from his wildness intact.

"Nora Kennedy was there," Merry added with a smile, remembering. Nora had looked good. Somehow she'd managed to keep herself unharmed despite the insanity. "And I got a lot of feelers for work. I was approached to do some set designing for a couple of videos."

"That sounds like fun."

Merry agreed, but she didn't know if she should accept or not. She would have to talk it over with John. Once she was done with his park, her job would probably be more part-time than full. If she suddenly left to do some other jobs, Jake's opinion that she was using his dad as a stepping-stone back into the business would be reinforced. She didn't want that. She wanted Jake's good opinion.

Her phone rang and she glanced at the caller ID. It was Jake. Should she answer? She reached out for her phone, her fingers trembling.

"Hello, Jake," she said, and watched her sister come to attention.

"Would you like to go to lunch? It's a beautiful day. We could head to Santa Monica pier. Maybe ride the new Ferris wheel."

Merry didn't hesitate. She agreed and he said he'd pick her up in an hour.

"Noelle, you have to go. Jake is on his way over to take me to lunch."

"Didn't he just leave?"

"Hours ago."

"You can't kick me out. I'm your sister."

"I'm kicking you out *because* you are my sister. Besides, don't you have a plane to catch?" Merry jumped to her feet, gathered up the coffeepot and the cups and carried them into the house. She had thirty minutes to shower and change.

The sun shone through the fronds of the palm trees lining the street as Jake put the Mercedes in Park and sat staring at Merry's front door. He hadn't planned on calling her for lunch so soon after... Well, after last night, but his hand had kept straying to his phone and finally he'd given in and called her to see if she had plans for lunch.

How could one woman have turned his life topsy-turvy in so short a time? He prided himself on his logical thinking, his ability to create order out of disorder. Was he just reliving his boyhood crush on her? She'd been his fantasy girl when he'd been in high school. With the reality of the fantasy at his fingertips, he wasn't certain what he liked more: the fact that he'd had a chance to relive his fantasy crush, or the fact that the living, breathing woman was so much more than his fantasy. Acts of irrationality bothered him since he so seldom had them, but Merry tempted him to throw caution to the wind and go with his instincts.

The curtain in her front window moved slightly, and he imagined her standing on the other side looking at him, wondering what he was doing. He had no answer. He didn't know what he was doing. He didn't even know why he'd called her on the spur of the moment and asked her out to lunch. He should have just enjoyed the sex and left, but he couldn't stay away from her. He wasn't the kind of man who took the sex and ran. The situation had turned uncomfortable, and he didn't like it.

A knock sounded on his window and he stumbled back to the present, unaware of how far away his thoughts had taken him. Merry peered at him through the glass. "Are you going to sit there all day?"

He opened the door and got out. She looked flushed and excited. She wore white pants and a dark blue top. She'd pulled her hair into a ponytail that curled across one shoulder.

"Sorry. I was just answering a text."

"With your mind?" she asked, one eyebrow raised. "Come on in. You look hot, and not in the fun way."

He followed her up the path to the front door. All the way, he couldn't take his eyes from the graceful line of her neck and the little ringlets of hair at the nape. He wanted to touch her, breathe in the subtle scent of her perfume. Hell, he wanted a repeat of last night. In fact, he wanted a lot of repeats.

The house was cool inside. She led the way to the kitchen and out the back to the patio, where a tray sat on a round patio table with two sweating glasses of iced tea.

"Sit down," she said. "We have to talk."

"About what?" he asked, before his mind fell into gear.

"Seriously?" she replied. "Is this really how you want to play it?"

"What about lunch?"

"It'll be delivered here in ten minutes. What we need to discuss shouldn't be aired over a restaurant table with strangers listening in."

She settled gracefully into the lawn chair and picked up her iced tea.

He didn't want tea. He didn't want lunch. He wanted her, on the bed, her body open to him. Images of the night before from the moment he'd removed her dress till the moment he'd fallen asleep with her in his arms returned to him so forcefully that heat surged in his groin.

"What happened last night... I mean, afterward..." He stumbled to a halt. He'd never had a problem with words before.

She tilted her head toward him, waiting patiently. "Go on," she finally said.

"How does one go about telling someone very special that he had a crush on her when she was this cute little actress on this kiddie show without sounding like a stalker?"

"You had a crush on me? You told me you just liked the show, that Chloe was a loyal friend to Maddie." She looked surprised. "I had no idea that behind those statements was a deeper feeling. Most of the time you've acted as though I have the plague or something."

"I had a crush on Chloe," he said slowly. Maybe he

should have just kept his mouth shut. Nothing he said was going to come out right.

"Oh," she said, disappointment in her tone. A small frown furrowed her forehead. "You're one of those. You'd think I'd learn. Usually I can smell a Chloe addict from a mile away."

"I don't… I don't mean…" He felt like he was back in high school, too tongue-tied to ask the girl he liked to the senior prom.

She held up her hand. "Stop. Is that what last night was all about? You were taking Chloe to the awards show so you could walk the red carpet with her and then bring her home and pretty much have a good ole time?"

"No… No…" He rubbed his temples. "I'm trying to say…"

"Wow," she said, sitting back in her chair. "This hasn't happened to me in a long time." She slanted a glance at him. "I feel a little betrayed. I thought you were paying attention to me, to Meredith Alcott."

How did this conversation get to this point? He was totally baffled. "You don't understand."

"I don't want to talk about it right now," she said, standing up, looking suddenly tired. The breeze ruffled her hair and a look of loss and disappointment shadowed her eyes. "Maybe you should go."

"Merry," he said.

"I need to be alone right now." She stared at him.

Did he see tears in the corners of her eyes? How the hell was he going to fix this? His opened his mouth to say something.

"Please, Jake," she repeated. "You know the way." She turned and walked into the house, slamming and locking the door.

He sat stunned, not certain what the hell had happened. Here he'd thought he'd tell her that he liked the real woman more than the fantasy, and not one word had come out right. He never would've brought the subject up.

His phone rang and he took it out of his pocket. His father. He considered not answering, but what the hell else could go wrong? He might as well get the next calamity over with.

"Jake," his father said, his voice breathless and hurried. "We have a problem."

"What's up, Dad?"

"Fire, and it's coming toward the park."

"I'm leaving Merry's home. Do you want me to tell her?"

He heard his father hesitate. "I want to speak to her myself. I'll call her as soon as I hang up with you."

"I'll be there as quick as I can." He skirted the house, following a small brick walkway that meandered through her garden. He got into his car and started it. He backed out of Merry's driveway, thinking he should have just knocked on the door and told her about the fire, but he didn't think he could face her just yet.

Merry couldn't believe a fire was threatening the park. She'd changed out of capris and her silk shirt into plain jeans and a cotton T-shirt. Even though John had told her to just stay home, she couldn't. She might not have as much invested in the park as he did, but she'd come to love it. She entered the freeway and gunned her Prius to merge into the fast-moving traffic. She could not bear the thought of that beautiful park burning down.

The worry about the fire receded in her mind as thoughts of Jake came to the forefront. *Dumb. Dumb. Dumb,* she thought. What was she going to do? Her earlier conversation with her sister had done little to help her.

She should never have slept with John's son. That had been asking for trouble. And now she was probably right behind him as they both raced to the park and the threatening fire. Though what she would do about the fire, she didn't know. What was she going to do about Jake? She didn't know that, either. Hell, she couldn't hang on to a thought. Just the sense of regret she'd felt when he'd confessed his crush on Chloe. She hadn't let her guard down with a man for a long time.

Today, she didn't seem to know much of anything. *Where was my brain?* she thought. *I'm smarter than this. I got my man merit badge a long time ago.*

She swerved as a car cut in front of her. She wanted to pound the steering wheel in frustration. She wanted to pound Jake in frustration. He was in the entertainment business. He understood how the fantasy worked. How could he think she was just an extension of her TV character? He was smarter than that. He should have gotten over being starstruck a long time ago. A man who saw the crazy in his celebrity clients should know better. Why would he even get involved with her when all he saw was the illusion?

Even with the air conditioner going, the smell of smoke filtered into the cab. More than one fire darkened the sky today, casting a yellow haze over the city. She turned on the radio and found three fires blazing and a city stressed out as mandatory evacuations were being ordered for those in the fires' paths. People thought Los Angeles was wall-to-wall people, but in reality there was still a lot of open land with vegetation that turned bone dry once the rainy season ended. A heavy rainy season meant more growth and a greater chance of fire.

Jake was an idiot. And the worst thing was, she was an idiot, too. She had let the glamour and romance of the evening sway her common sense. She should never have invited him in for a drink. She should never have unlocked her front door. She should never have let him kiss her the first time. She should never... Her mind skittered around her thoughts.

Once this fire thing was cleared up, she would finish what she started. John wouldn't need her to be at the park every day once the restoration was done and the park redesigned with the seasonal displays laid out. She would probably be able to work at home and go to the park to consult with John. Then she could do some work on the side. Maybe one of the video offers would pan out.

An hour later, she pulled into the parking lot and parked next to John's Mercedes. The pall of black smoke made her cough. A few cinders swirled around her head. The wind was a roar that snapped at her hair. She could smell smoke, and when she shaded her eyes she could see fire trucks on distant hillsides and firefighters in full gear. A tanker plane roared overhead, circled the burn area and a few moments later dropped fire retardant on the flames.

She heard the roar of a bulldozer and watched as it wheeled across the parking lot. Jake was driving it, a yellow hard hat on his head, his face firm with determination. She didn't wave as she bolted across the hot tarmac and into the park. John was in the center courtyard with all the maintenance people.

"We're going to bulldoze as much of the vegetation beyond the easement as far from the park perimeter as we can get before the flames get here," he said. "I want two teams. Mark, you and your people water down the roofs of the stores. Jose, you and your team work around the carousel. Keep everything as wet as you can. Don't worry about water, we're on a well."

"What can I do, John?" Merry asked as she approached.

"I don't know, Merry." He looked calm, but panic hovered in his eyes. He turned to gaze at the hills where the flames flickered.

Merry imagined she could hear the crackle, even though the fire was still several miles away.

A line of cars following a fire truck turned into the parking lot. As the cars parked, people started getting out and walking toward John. Firemen opened the side panels in the truck and began to unroll hoses and attach them to the fire hydrants.

"Merry," John said suddenly. "I want you to go into my office and your office and save all the computers you can and your plans for the park. Pack them in your car. If we lose anything, we'll still have our plans."

Merry nodded. She passed a knot of people half running toward John. She recognized the woman, Bonnie, who owned the pub. "We came to help, John," she said.

Other people nodded. They were all dressed in old clothes, holding shovels and chainsaws, ready to fight the fire. A few had tied wet bandannas across their faces to filter out the smoke.

"I can't ask you to help, Bonnie," John said, his tone serious. "You're civilians. The fire department is going to want you out of the way."

"We're not leaving. This park is an icon and I'm not going to let it burn down. My parents brought me here when I was a child and I bring my children," Bonnie said firmly.

"Me, too, John." A man Merry didn't know spoke up. "I worked the concession stands three summers in a row and that money helped me through college. I'm not going to let this park burn down if I can help it."

As John started organizing Bonnie and her friends,

more cars poured into the parking lot and more people rushed up to John with shovels over their shoulders. John had a bemused look on his face. Jake had parked the bulldozer and was talking to a fireman and a police officer. He kept glancing at the crowd around his father.

Merry watched him. He raised an arm and pointed to the side of the park. Though the park was required to have a vegetation-free easement, it was still vulnerable. Flames had been known to leap across eight lanes of highway.

Merry went into her office and started packing up her laptop, along with all her drawing pads, her notes and her schedule of events. She packed up her car and then went back to John's office for his laptops. John loved computers and not only had a Mac, an iPod and an iPad, but two PCs and a couple of dozen flash drives. She found a box for the flash drives and dropped them in. Then she started unhooking all the power supplies and closing the laptops. How John could work on so many different computers at once mystified her.

The door opened behind her and she turned to find Jake standing in the doorway, his yellow hard hat still on his head and a soaking-wet bandanna in his hand.

"What the hell are you doing?" he asked.

"Your dad told me to get all the computers, so I'm getting them and putting them in my car."

"You should be home where you'd be safe."

"Thanks," she said, her voice vacant of any snark. "But I'm not leaving. I'm going to help all I can." She owed it to John.

"This is dangerous."

"Life is dangerous. I just braved the freeway going eighty miles an hour. Fighting a fire is nothing. Are you going to run away?"

His face tightened. "This is my dad's life."

"It's mine, too." She wanted him to go away, to leave her to her task. Looking at him brought the hurt back, and she didn't know if she wanted to smack him or kiss him. "Go do what you have to do. Let me do my job. We will deal with this later."

He stomped out into the smoke and Merry slammed the door after him. When she finished with the computers, she headed to Noelle's store to see what she could save and found Connor Bentley, the mayor, inside already packing.

"Mr. Mayor," Merry said in surprise. "What are you doing here?"

"Merry." He wrapped newspaper around a glass piece and set it carefully in one of the blue totes Noelle used to transport her glass. "Are you here to help? Take this." He handed her a glass bowl.

"You're the mayor. Should you be putting yourself in jeopardy? I should think you'd have people to do this for you."

"I know your sister is on her way to San Francisco. I had to make some effort to save her product. It's…it's just too beautiful." He gazed at a glass butterfly that looked as though it was ready to fly away.

"Yeah," Merry said, trying to keep her surprise down. Was the mayor sweet on her sister? *Good Lord, I don't have time for this.* "Concentrate on the top two shelves. That's the expensive stuff. The smaller items are easier and faster to redo if they're lost."

Connor nodded and reached up to bring the larger, more expensive pieces down. Merry wrapped newspaper around them. Through the window, she saw Mark with his crew hosing down the roofs. Streams of water dripped along the eaves. The smoke was getting thicker and heavier. More sirens sounded as more fire trucks and firefighters arrived.

"I'm going to get my truck and just drive it up here to the door and we'll pack this away. Then we can start on the T-shirt shop and save as much as we can."

Merry simply nodded. He opened the door and a burst of smoke nearly choked her as it swirled in. The wind had died down a bit, but glowing cinders continued to swirl and litter the central courtyard. One of Mark's crew watered down the cinders before something caught fire.

The fire was closer. Merry stood in the doorway shading her eyes. She heard the distant crackle and felt a touch of primal fear. Everything about fire was frightening to her.

Connor parked his truck in front of Noelle's store and Merry helped him load the totes. The T-shirt shop hadn't unpacked any boxes yet, so Merry helped put them in his truck. When it was loaded, he drove away. Merry watched him turn onto the road and roar off.

The smoke grew heavier and the air was harder to breathe. Merry coughed as she wet down a bandanna to tie around her face.

"Ma'am," said a firefighter, "you need to leave now."

She hadn't noticed the fire was almost to the park. Hundreds of people worked tirelessly, but the fire was getting too close. Merry closed her eyes, trying not to cry.

"Merry," Jake said. He'd parked the bulldozer and climbed down to stand next to her. "The roller coaster is on fire."

"Your dad was thinking about a new one." Merry walked to the edge of the walkway and stared at the flames consuming the bracing on the roller coaster.

"You're pretty calm about it."

"I worked with Maddie Blake and she set at least one

thing on fire every week. I carried my own fire extinguisher." John was herding people toward the parking
lot. He looked so dejected, Merry wanted to put her arms
around him. Everything he'd worked for was likely to
be gone in a minute.

"Merry," Jake said, "it's time to leave."

"But…"

"The insurance will cover this. Dad will be able to
rebuild."

"If he wants."

"I'm not risking your life over the park."

John stood at the edge of the parking lot, staring at
the fire. The flames weren't as high and fierce as they
had been before, but the embers were hot.

"Bonnie is serving meals for everyone at the pub. Go
on and I'll meet you there."

Merry nodded. She didn't want to leave, but even she
could see that nothing she did anymore would make a
difference. She skirted fire engines parked helter-skelter
in the lot and made her weary way to her car. A glance
at the clock on the dash told her it was nearly six. She'd
been here for over six hours and realized she'd eaten
nothing since breakfast.

Tears rolled down her cheeks as she watched the park
recede into the distance, eventually swallowed completely by the yellow smoky haze.

Chapter 11

The pub was crowded with the people who had worked to help save the park. Despite the crowd, very little talk occurred. Everyone watched the TV mounted over the bar. A commentator showed the flames and gave a history of the park. An aerial view showed the roller coaster in flames and firefighters blasting it with water.

"Sad," Bonnie said as she seated Merry at a table. Bonnie poured water into a glass.

"So far it looks like the fire is winning."

"Maybe," Bonnie said, and sat down across from Merry. "I've been trying to remember where I knew you from. Took me a bit, but I finally remembered."

"Maddie's Mad World," Merry supplied for her.

Bonnie laughed. "You get that a lot, don't you?"

Merry simply nodded.

"Well, you're in good hands with Jake. He'll get you

back on your feet. He's brilliant at what he does. There's no shame."

For a moment, Merry didn't understand what she was saying. "I beg your pardon?"

Bonnie simply laughed. "We all thought the money would last forever."

"No," Merry said, "I'm not Jake's client."

Bonnie tilted her head. "Oh, goodness. I assumed because you were here with Jake, you were broke and…"

Merry held up a hand. "It's okay. I'm not broke. My mother is really shrewd about money. She would never have let me live like the money would last forever."

Bonnie grinned. "Your mother didn't go to the celebrity mother school of behavior."

"Not even," Merry said.

"Count your blessings," Bonnie said with a sigh and a sad look in her eyes. "My family couldn't spend my money fast enough. If not for Jake, I'd be living under a bridge like my troll of an ex-husband."

Merry took a long sip of her water. Bonnie refilled the glass. "You look hungry. Hamburgers are on the house today."

"I'm starving. I haven't eaten since breakfast."

Jake entered the pub and saw Merry and Bonnie. He walked over and Bonnie stood to give him her spot in the booth.

"I need about ten glasses of water, Bonnie," he said.

"Coming right up." Bonnie went to get more glasses and then left the pitcher of water for them.

"What's happening at the park?"

"It looks like the only casualty is going to be the roller coaster. The wind shifted at the last moment and the fire went north."

Merry breathed a sigh of relief and said a little prayer

of thanks. "So you're going to get a new roller coaster and the insurance is going to pay for it. Considering that your father was going to build a new one anyway, boy, that's a win-win situation."

Jake grinned at her. He downed a glass of water. "And some new landscaping. Two of your Christmas displays were lost, too."

"I don't care about the displays. The park has been saved."

A cheer went up from the bar as the commentator on the TV announced the park to be safe and the fire 60 percent contained. An aerial view showed the fire leaping north of the park. The roller coaster was still burning, but the rides nearby were safe. Including the carousel. Firefighters moved through the park, spraying water on the areas along the perimeter and putting out embers. Planes dropped fire retardant on the flames.

Bonnie came out with two plates and set them in front of Merry and Jake. Merry eyed her hamburger hungrily. She picked up a French fry and bit into it. Heavenly. Bonnie made terrific fries and the hamburger smelled as delicious as it looked.

Jake bit hungrily into his hamburger. "This is good," he said.

Merry dug in to hers. For a few moments, she and Jake ate in silence. The pub had grown noisier now that the fire was almost vanquished and all the volunteers seemed to be feeling happier.

"About this morning," Jake said and paused, eyeing her.

"I don't want to talk about it yet," Merry said, still hurting and angry.

"But…"

She held up her hand. "No. Not now."

The door to the pub opened and John walked in. He looked exhausted, but he was smiling. A few cheers sounded and he waved, shaking hands and thanking every person in the room for their help.

Merry watched him, feeling a sense of pride. John had created his own community and she liked that she was part of it, too. He made his way around the room and finally found his way to Jake and Merry. Jake shifted to make room for his father.

John put his hands over his face.

"The park is saved," Merry said. "We can fix it."

"I know, Merry," John said with a deep sigh. "But the real problem right now is that the fire may have been arson."

"Arson!" A look of incredulity spread across Jake's face.

"Yes, arson," John replied. "And the police questioned me as though I had something to do with it."

Merry shook her head. "No."

"Why would you torch the park after you spent so much money to renovate?" Jake looked like he wanted to hit something.

John looked sad and pensive. Tension tightened the edges of his mouth. "I think I convinced them of that. But the fire was positioned to head straight for the park. If not for the wind change, everything would have been lost and I would have been forced to sell no matter what I wanted."

"Yeah, the insurance company isn't going to pay out if you're the arsonist."

"I'm not," John said quietly. "I came to find you because I need my laptop."

"They're all in my car. Which one do you want?"

"The Mac," he said with a little smile.

* * *

The door opened and Jake looked up, expecting to
see Merry. His sister, Evelyn, stormed into the pub. She
was smartly dressed in a dark gray suit and a yellow
silk blouse, with a gray-and-yellow scarf tied around
her neck. Her black hair was pulled back into a severe
knot at the top of her head. She obviously had just come
from a class.

"I can see you're all fine." Evelyn's tone was clipped
and angry. "Thank God. And I heard on the radio that
the fire is moving away from the park. How nice it would
have been if someone had called me." She sat down
across from them in Merry's spot.

Jake flinched. Evelyn angry was the last thing he
needed.

"Sorry, kitten," John said. "Everything happened so
quickly. I didn't want to worry you, especially with midterms coming up." He took her hand in his and gently
patted it until she pulled away.

She shoved Merry's plate out of the way, her eyes narrowing as she rested her arms on the table, staring at both
of them. "I have a T.A. who worries about midterms."

John glanced at Jake, and Jake tried not to squirm.
Evelyn on a rant was a sight to behold.

"If you had just sold the property to whoever wanted
it, you wouldn't need to be worried about a little fire like
that. The developers would probably have been delighted
if everything had just burned. They wouldn't have to dis-
mantle all the buildings and the rides."

And she wouldn't have to worry about her son wanting to be part of the future of the park when she wanted
him to be a lawyer, or a doctor or president of the United
States.

"Evelyn," John said in a soothing tone.

"Don't 'Evelyn' me in that tone of voice." She tapped her fingertips on the table angrily. "You were both in danger and didn't think I should be worried."

Jake flinched at the sarcasm in her voice.

"We were kind of hoping you wouldn't know." John tried to smile, but his lips didn't quite stretch into one. Like Jake, he was intimidated by his overachieving daughter, who was determined she'd be head of the physics department by the time she was forty.

"The fire was on every news station. Hell, one of the newscasters talked about how he met his wife at the park and still brought his children."

"How nice," Jake said, taking a long sip of water.

"So I rushed over. I knew you'd all gather here."

Bonnie came over. "Evelyn," she exclaimed happily. "What a close thing. But we all worked at diverting the fire and the park has been saved."

"So I heard. The newscaster on Channel Five talked about how people from the community turned out to fight the fire. He was so amazed that anyone would turn out for a run-down park like that."

"Run-down?" John said. "You haven't been out there recently. Merry has done a terrific job with the redecorating."

"The has-been actress."

Jake took offense at Evelyn's statement. "I'm done listening to you. Dad made his decision. You can either support it or not. But you will not, under any circumstances, denigrate anyone he sees fit to hire. Just because you and I didn't want the park doesn't mean there aren't other people who think it's something worth saving. You have no idea how many people showed up to help fight the fire. You and I have forgotten how beloved this park is and what it means to the people of Riverside."

Evelyn stared at him, her lips parted and surprise on her face. "The park is a menace, a money pit and a…"

"Don't talk to your father and brother like that," Merry said, tapping Evelyn on the shoulder.

Jake hadn't even seen her approach. She held a tote in one hand, the corners of his dad's Mac and iPad peeking out.

"Excuse me?" Evelyn said icily.

"He's trying to save a piece of Riverside history," Merry continued. "Move over, my hamburger is getting cold."

Evelyn slid over in the booth. Merry handed the tote to John then sat down, pulling her plate toward her.

"You are not part of this family," Evelyn said, ice forming on each word.

"Maybe not the biological part," Merry said. "I'm family in a different way."

Evelyn glared at her father. "Are you going to let this has-been actress talk to me like this?"

"She's defending me," John replied. "Why should I stop her?"

"Okay, everybody," Jake said, "neutral corners. And Evelyn, if you keep talking like this, the arson investigator is going be knocking on your door."

"Arson!" Evelyn drew back. "Someone tried to burn you down, Dad? It wasn't an accident? Who would do something like that?" Her tone softened with worry.

John shrugged. "I don't know, Evelyn. I just know that evidence of some sort was found at the ignition site and the cops spent a bit of time talking to me."

"You wouldn't burn down your own park," Evelyn said, apprehension showing in her eyes and the lines forming on her forehead. "Dad, please tell me the police don't suspect you."

"Right now, they suspect everyone, but me in particular. And according to you, I'm holding on to a rundown park. Which could make you a suspect, too," John said wearily.

"I was in class all morning," she said stiffly, "and I have a whole list of people who can verify that."

"Evelyn, I was just teasing." John rubbed his temples, tension radiating from him.

Evelyn caved, her shoulders slumping and tears forming in the corners of her eyes. "Dad. Jake. I'm sorry. When I heard about the fire, I was just so frightened for you both. And when you didn't call me…"

"It's all right, dear," John said, patting her hand again. "I apologize for not letting you know we were all right."

Now that most of the volunteers had been fed and rehydrated, many had drifted home to be replaced by the early-evening crowd. The smell of smoke lingered in the air and Jake realized he smelled of smoke, too.

Merry had finished her hamburger and fries and was draining another glass of water. She looked exhausted.

Evelyn opened her mouth as though to say something, but nothing came out. She shook her head and wiped away the tears. "I'm sorry for being difficult. I was just worried."

"We understand, sis," Jake said. He loved his sister despite her slightly overbearing, type-A personality.

Defeated, Evelyn plucked an uneaten French fry off Jake's plate and chewed on it. That surprised him. She was all about healthy eating, and fries did not figure into that equation.

"I guess I need to be getting home. Johnny is going to be worried about me and the park if he's heard the news."

Jake's phone rang and he tugged it out of his pocket.

"Harry Constantine," he said to his father. "Jake Walters here."

"I hear you're having a fire problem," Constantine said.

"Crisis averted. The fire is under control. The only ride lost was the roller coaster, which was coming down anyway."

"That's good news." Constantine's voice held a note of false sincerity. "I'm renewing my offer to purchase the property."

"For a lower price, I assume." Jake tried to keep his voice neutral, but the man's manner just grated on him.

"No, not at all. I've been instructed by my investors to sweeten the offer a bit more. Say another five hundred thousand dollars. You won't get another offer this generous for years."

"Now is not the time, Mr. Constantine." How interesting that Harry Constantine would be making another offer just now, especially with the suspicion of arson.

"This is the perfect time. Think about how many jobs a new mall would generate in Riverside. The economy is improving by leaps and bounds. There's a profit to be made here. A lot of profit. I can smell it."

Jake resisted the urge to disconnect on the man. But he kept thinking that the money from the sale would make his dad secure for the rest of his life. Jake didn't deal in risk. His clients were risky, but he couldn't be risky with their money. If one of his clients had a deal like this come up, Jake would have accepted it, no questions asked. He'd orchestrated estate sales for clients who were in dire straights. Though his dad was a long way from being destitute, Jake worried that that could change at any time. He wanted his dad to be protected.

Part of him wished the park had burned down. Then

he wouldn't have to deal with this issue. The park would be sold and his dad would be sitting on his boat drinking margaritas. Besides, he and Evelyn were his dad's back-up plan, and Jake didn't mind that. Then again, a lot of people would be out of a job. And those people who had turned out to help fight the fire would translate to a whole lot of ticket sales once the renovation was done and the park reopened.

How did he balance what was best for his dad and what his dad wanted? John Walters was committed to the park. Jake wasn't.

"Mr. Constantine, I'll relay your offer to my father. But I can pretty much guarantee he's not going to sell." He disconnected, not wanting to talk to Constantine any longer.

"What did he say?" Merry asked curiously.

"Just repeating his offer to purchase the park." Jake studied her. As long as the park was going forward, he got to be with Merry. And he wanted to be with her. Suddenly, he knew he was completely in favor of the renovations if it kept Merry in his life. He wanted to be near her. He wanted to be as important to her as she was to him.

Evelyn frowned as she took another French fry from Jake's plate. "At least we know he's still interested."

"This isn't the right time, Evelyn." Jake drank another glass of water and then leaned back against the booth. "I just want to go home, get a shower and sleep for twenty-four hours."

"We all smell of smoke," Merry said.

Evelyn wrinkled her nose. "You do smell bad."

John pushed himself heavily to his feet. He tucked his laptop under his arm. "I'll see you on Monday."

Merry stood and Evelyn got out and tucked her hand

around her father's arm. She walked out with him without saying goodbye.

"We need to talk," Jake said.

"The only talking I'm going to do is with my pillow." Merry smothered a yawn. She looked so tired Jake wanted to hold her.

"I really want to clear something up. I said some things this morning and they didn't come out right. I want to explain."

"I'm tired, I'm cranky and I smell. Can we talk tomorrow?"

"Sure." Jake nodded.

"Come by tomorrow for lunch and we'll talk. Lunch is on me." She pushed herself to her feet and started for the door.

Jake flagged Bonnie down. "How much do we owe?" He gestured at the room and the few volunteers still left.

"Your dad already took care of the bill," she said. "Go home and get some rest. You look beat." She turned and headed back toward the bar.

Jake rubbed his eyes. They felt gritty with smoke and exhaustion. Then he walked out the door only to find two men in dark suits standing at the curb. They glanced at him as he walked out into the heavy evening air, which still smelled sour with the smoke from all the fires. No breeze freshened the night and the staleness seemed to lay on everything.

"Mr. Walters," one of the men said.

Jake paused, an eyebrow raised. "Can I help you?"

Each man held up their badge for Jake to see. "I'm Detective Steven Mars and this is my partner, Detective Miles Pederson. We're with the arson investigations. We'd like to talk to you about the fire."

Jake nodded. He'd been expecting them.

"We spoke with your father earlier," Detective Mars said. "We have reason to believe the fire was arson. And the way the fire was started, it was pointed directly at the park. Do you know anyone who would gain from the destruction of the park?"

Jake studied the two men. "Hurt the park? No. As I was reminded today, the park is a Riverside icon. A lot of people showed up to help us fight the fire."

"Wasn't the park up for sale earlier this year?"

"Yes, but Dad changed his mind and decided to renovate instead."

Detective Mars smiled. "My parents took me there when I was a kid and someday, when I have kids, I'm hoping to take them, too."

"I don't know what to say, Detectives. I'm baffled. I'm having a hard enough time believing it was arson and that anyone would want to destroy the park."

"Can you tell us who made the offers on the park?"

"I can't imagine anyone wanting to get that land so badly they'd be willing to risk hurting people."

"You'd be surprised at what people will do," Detective Pederson said. "Trust me, nothing surprises me anymore."

"The main offer came from Harry Constantine. He has a team of investors who've been trying to buy the land for a number of years now. He wants to build a mall. I checked him out because he seemed the most interested, but in reality he's a vulture. He doesn't have any money problems, so I don't think he'd be desperate enough to start fire.

"And then the Kessler Corporation made an offer. They build houses. But this land is zoned for commercial development and getting it changed would take time. I really don't think they were that interested." Jake didn't think they were as interested in the land as they had been in Constantine's offer. A strong rivalry had existed between the two groups for years.

"I don't remember the name of the contact, but I have it in my office." Jake paused to think. "And Kyle Potter Inc. Mr. Potter's lawyer tendered the offer. My dad and I don't like the way they do business, so we never followed through on their offer. And there were a few other inquiries, but nothing that interested us."

Pederson made notes in a small spiral notebook, nodding as he wrote. "Anyone have a personal grudge against your father?"

Jake couldn't think of one person who would hate his father enough to set fire to the park. "Not that I know of. My father dealt with every complaint personally. I don't think anyone ever went home angry after a day in the park. I don't know what else I can tell you, Detectives."

Detective Mars handed him a business card. "If you think of anything else, please let us know."

"What did you find that made you think it was arson?" Jake asked.

"We found a crude incendiary device. It's at the lab now for analysis."

"Thank you, Detectives. If I remember anything, I'll let you know. Do you have any suspects?"

"It's too early in the investigation to have any solid information. We're still gathering facts."

Merry stepped out of the shower. The sun shone in her bathroom window, which was cracked open to let out the steam. This was her third shower, and she imagined she still smelled like smoke. She dried her hair and pulled a strand to her nose to sniff, satisfied that the smell of smoke was finally gone.

She dressed in her best jeans and red silk blouse. She checked her makeup. Everything was perfect. She wanted to look hot, but not as if she'd put a lot of work into it. She was just heading into the kitchen when the doorbell rang. She opened it, expecting Jake, only to find two strange men standing on her front porch looking very grave.

"Miss Alcott," one of the men said. "I'm Detective Steven Mars and this is Detective Miles Pederson. May we speak to you about the fire yesterday at the park?"

She stood aside to let them in. "I was just about to make coffee. Would you like some?"

They followed her to the kitchen.

Oh, my God. Oh, my God. Why were they questioning her? She went through the motions of making coffee, and when it was dripping into the carafe, she turned and tried to smile.

"I remember you," Miles Pederson said. *"Maddie's Mad World.* My sister never missed an episode."

Merry smiled. There were times when being recognized didn't make her feel good. This was one of those times. She poured coffee in mugs to hide the trembling in her hands.

"I had fun on the show," Merry said as she handed a mug to each detective. She sat down at the kitchen table and sipped her own coffee.

"I worked at Glendale," Detective Pederson said, "when Maddie and you were caught joyriding in that stolen car."

Merry covered her face. Great, the worst moment of her life and this cop had to remember it. "I was fifteen and I didn't know it was stolen." What were they saying? Did they suspect her of setting the fire because she'd been caught in a stolen car with Maddie driving? She'd been in a world of hurt after that incident. Her mother and father had grounded her for two months and made her donate her pay from one episode to charity. And here she was hoping she'd finally lived it down.

The detective laughed. "Yeah, you shocked the hell out of me and my partner. We thought you were the ultimate good girl."

"And you are remembering the worst incident of my life while I've been trying to forget it."

He chuckled again. "I can understand that." His demeanor changed. "So about the fire yesterday…"

"Mr. Walters talked to me and said you thought it was arson. I didn't have anything to do with it. I was here with Jake when Mr. Walters called." Actually, she was home, and Jake had been sitting in his car in the driveway while she fumed. Just when she was starting to really like him.

"We're just gathering information," Detective Mars said. "You make good coffee. Care to give some pointers to my wife?"

Merry offered hopefully, "It's Starbucks Sumatra French press."

The detective nodded. "Do you know anyone who might have a reason to torch the park?"

She sipped her coffee, giving herself time to think. Jake hadn't been happy about his father's decision to not sell, but he would never set fire to the park. He respected his father too much. "No, not really. I've only worked there a few months."

"We heard that Jake Walters wasn't happy with his father's decision to renovate the park."

"In the beginning. Jake wanted his father to retire and take life easy, but the park means everything to Mr. Walters. Jake would never do anything to harm him. He respects his father and his father's decisions."

Detective Mars nodded. "But still, a guy's got to be a little worried that that money pit will dip into his inheritance."

"I will be the first to say that Jake wants to know where every penny goes, and I have to give him three good reasons why it went there, but he didn't start the fire."

"People do things for reasons you'll never understand."

"There you're wrong. I worked with Maddie Jefferson. I worked in the entertainment business long enough. I can smell crazy. Jake Walters is as steady as a rock. And trust me, he may disagree with his father, but he would do nothing to hurt him. And frankly, I don't know anyone at the park who would, either. Mr. Walters is loved by everyone. Whoever set the fire had to be someone from the outside."

"Like who?"

"I wouldn't know how to find out. I've never played a detective. Though there was an episode on *Maddie's Mad World* where I had to find out who had stolen the school hamster." She'd loved that episode. Maddie had been in the hospital after having her tonsils removed and Merry had gotten to be the star. The script had been rewritten for her, and she'd loved that fact that for once she was the center of attention.

"Thank you," Detective Pederson said, closing his notebook and tucking it away inside his jacket pocket. "We appreciate your time. If we have any further questions, we'll be in contact. If you remember anything, here's my card."

She took the business card. "I'm sorry I couldn't be more help."

"Actually, you were very helpful," Detective Peder-

son said. Then he cleared his throat and looked a bit uncomfortable. "Could I ask you for your autograph? My
sister will be thrilled."

"Of course," she replied, getting up. "And your sister's name is...?"

"Susan Fields," he supplied.

She went into the office where she kept a few photos
for the times when someone actually asked her for one.
She signed her name with a flourish and added *to Susan*
at the top. Usually people asked her if she could get them
Maddie's autograph.

She walked the detectives to the front door and then
stood in the living room to watch them drive off. She
turned to head back into the kitchen, but another car, a
black Cadillac Escalade, turned into her driveway and
parked. Daryl Wicks stepped out and her eyebrows went
up in surprise. He held a bouquet of flowers in one hand
and a box in the other. What did he want?

Merry met Daryl at the door, opening it just as his
finger was poised to ring the doorbell.

"Daryl, what brings you here?"

He smiled at her. "May I come in?"

She glanced down the street and tried not to look too
worried. "I'm expecting someone."

"This will only take a moment. I brought you flowers." He handed her the bouquet. "And candy." He looked
a little uncertain over the candy as he handed her the
box, as though it was a bit much.

She took the box. She was never one to turn down
chocolate. She glanced at the box. Lenoux of Beverly
Hills was emblazoned across the gold foil of the lid.
Wow, this chocolate was five hundred dollars a pound.
Even when she could afford it, she didn't spend so much
on candy. But she could feel the tender chocolates call-

ing her name. She was so going to be alone with this box tonight.

"Thank you."

"I couldn't stop thinking about you after Friday night." He walked into the house, looking around curiously.

Yeah, right, she thought. She was the one who got away and he was remembering the rejection. "Thank you for the flowers and the candy, but you shouldn't have. Why are you here?"

"Seeing you Friday night got me thinking about the old days."

She laughed. "You make it sound like we grew up in the Middle Ages."

"In the entertainment industry, it kind of was." He looked thoughtful. "Back in those days, I could sing what I wanted to sing, be who I wanted to be. No one had any expectations of me."

She tilted her head up at him. "You've been at the top of an industry that spits out new people every three months. And you've managed to remain on top for a long time."

"I give people what they want. Not necessarily what I want."

She sighed. She could see he wasn't ready to leave. "Do you want some coffee?"

"Thank you. I would."

She led the way to the kitchen. "So what are you saying exactly?" She poured coffee into a clean mug and handed it to him.

"Back then, I was the person I wanted to be."

A jerk, she thought. "Are you feeling sorry for yourself?" And here she was thinking he was still interested in her; in reality he was thinking about himself.

"No. That would be ridiculous." He walked around

her large, open kitchen looking at the decor. "I'm feeling nostalgic."

"So you bring me beautiful flowers and expensive chocolate because you're feeling nostalgic?"

He shrugged. "I kind of feel like I didn't apologize to you for the way I acted."

"You wrote a song about me."

"You're still not impressed with me, are you?"

She laughed. The doorbell rang again. Jake! She didn't want to deal with him. She opened the door, aware of Daryl standing behind her.

"Jake," she said brightly. "Hi. I meant to call you, because Daryl is taking me out to lunch."

"Excuse me?"

"What?" Daryl said. "Yeah, right. We have reservations at The Ivy."

Jake scowled, staring hard at Daryl. "Really. The Ivy?"

"Yeah," Merry said, suddenly not sure she was doing the right thing.

"I didn't know you wanted to be seen."

"They have great burgers."

"Then I'll see you tomorrow," Jake said.

"Goodbye. I'll be in bright and early." She closed the door and she turned to Daryl, feeling a little foolish.

Amusement showed in his face. "I haven't been the other man in a long time."

She tried to make her voice sound casual. "Jake and I aren't seeing each other."

"Does Jake know that?"

"Whatever," she said. "Are you really taking me to The Ivy?"

"I am now." He held out his arm.

Good, she thought, because she was going to drink

her lunch, so she wouldn't have to deal with the situation. After all, Daryl was business, and she had to think about her future.

Chapter 12

Jake sat at his desk, drumming his fingers while he looked at a photo on one of the celebrity sites with a Who Was Spotted Where column. Merry sat across from Daryl, looking so delectable that Jake wanted to punch his computer. She seemed to be gazing adoringly at the man who was gazing just as ardently back at her.

Jake ground his teeth. He scrolled to the next photo, showing them laughing, and the next photo, where they were clinking their wineglasses.

Meredith Alcott, not seen in years, found at The Ivy with Daryl Wicks, who composed the platinum hit song "Life After Merry." Are these two getting back together? And is Meredith Alcott trying to revive her career? We'll be following this story, so check back for more.

He glanced out the window to see if Merry had arrived yet. Her parking spot was empty. He went back to reading, trying to keep his runaway emotions under control. He couldn't believe he was upset. Why was he upset?

His father entered his office. "You're in early."

"There's a lot to do if you're going open in a couple of weeks."

"Yeah. I have a construction crew coming in to tear down the rest of the roller coaster. It's too dangerous to leave up. They should be here soon." John looked tired and worn. "I've been on the phone since I arrived with the insurance company, and then the police called wanting to see me again. I'm heading there in a moment."

"They talked to me, too, Saturday night. Do you want me to come with you?"

John's voice was thick with tension. "No need. Charles Bigelow is meeting me at police headquarters. I'll be fine, Jake."

"I know you will." Though Jake couldn't help a small worry that wormed its way through his thoughts.

"Do you have any idea who might have set the fire?" his father asked as he walked across the office.

"I'm an accountant. My first instinct is to follow the money. And, unfortunately, you have incredibly good insurance."

"The two detectives keep asking me about it. I've had the policy for forty years. If they really do suspect me, they should be wondering why I didn't burn it down at the peak of the market seven years ago when the land value was twice what it is now."

"I didn't know you had a criminal mind, Dad."

John didn't say anything. He just looked tired and stressed. "I saw Merry on the internet today. Something about her having lunch with this famous rap star. He's not one of your clients, is he?"

"He doesn't need me." Merry didn't need him, either.

"Good," John said. "Merry needs a nice young man."

Jake could hear the sarcasm is his father's voice. "I agree with you."

"Right. I'll believe that when the moon turns to green cheese."

"Aren't you worried she's trying to revive her career and leave you stuck with her project half-done?"

"You really like her, don't you? I like her, too, and I know she isn't going to leave me in a lurch." He gave Jake a shrewd, almost calculating look.

"You've always been a good judge of character, but this time I think you missed the mark." Jake tried not to squirm under his father's scrutiny.

"Nope, but I think you have."

After his father left, Jake found himself too restless to sit. He walked out into the mild morning air. The smell of smoke and burned timber was so thick he coughed. The park looked sad, with smoke stains clinging to the buildings and ash whirling in the breeze. With the fire completely out, he could breathe a sigh of relief, but the cleanup was going to be a twenty-four hour job.

He didn't hear Merry approach until she spoke. "With a lot of soap and water and a bit of pain, it will all look as good as new."

Jake turned to find her standing just behind him. "You're here."

"I'm here."

"I saw photos of you and Daryl on the internet this morning."

"We had a nice lunch." She rubbed at a sooty spot. "I really have to apologize for getting our signals crossed."

Jake didn't think they'd got their signals crossed. "Were the hamburgers as good as you remembered?"

She smiled slightly. "Better."

"And are you planning a career move?"

"And leave your dad? No." She gazed up at him, and something on her face made him want to kiss her. He wanted to do something that would make her forget Daryl Wicks. But then again, how did he compete with a megamillionaire who composed songs for the entertainment elite and whose fans could fill an entire stadium?

An emotion crossed her face, then was gone. Was that a bit of guilt? He looked more closely, but her face had turned bland. Nothing there, but still he felt a tiny glimmer of hope.

"I need to get my crew working and find my paintbrush," Merry said. "We have a lot of work to do. We'll talk later. 'Bye." She walked away, her hips swaying in time with her ponytail.

Jake's phone vibrated. Kessler Corporation. He closed his eyes. He didn't want to field another call about the fire. He answered it anyway.

"Alicia Mortensen," Jake said. "How are you?"

"I'm fine. I'm calling about the fire. Has your father changed his mind about selling?"

"No."

"My office put a lot of time and effort into our proposal. We've decided to give you another chance to accept it. This would get you out from under the burden of rebuilding. Let's face it. It's so run-down that nothing you're going to do will ever make it profitable again."

And this is your selling point, Jake thought. No one wants to be told their dream was so stale it was not revivable. "You're the last person on earth we would sell to after this conversation."

"Excuse me?"

"Rule number one of sales. Never make the seller feel like an idiot."

"Is there a rule number two?"

"Yeah, refer back to rule number one. Have a nice day, Miss Mortensen."

"You're going to regret this."

"I'm already sorry I talked to you in the first place." Jake disconnected and shoved his phone back into his pocket. Alicia Mortensen, Harry Constantine and the others who were swirling around his father to take advantage of his misfortune were all vultures. This was not unexpected, and he wouldn't be surprised if he had a few more offers for the property. Especially if they thought his father would just dump and run instead of dealing with the disaster.

He regretted ever trying to talk his dad into selling. He was glad he and his dad were okay. Something in his life had to be good, since he figured he'd lost Merry. Nothing he said was going to repair their relationship, as slight as it was. She didn't want anything to do with him.

Putting Noelle's shop back in order was easy enough. Connor had shown up to help her, and had just left to take the T-shirt stock back to its store, where the owner was waiting.

Noelle placed the pieces back on the displays while Merry unwrapped them and handed them to her.

"You seem a little tense today. How can you be tense after that exquisite lunch you had yesterday with Daryl, voted one of the sexiest men alive?"

"Maybe it's just me, but you seem to have a bit of a tone there." Her sister sounded accusatory. Merry felt guilty enough without her sister adding to it.

"Who, me? I don't have any idea what you're talking about." Noelle set a glass grizzly bear on a shelf and then moved it back and forth until she was satisfied with the position.

"Jake came right out and told me he had a crush on Chloe. In fact, the first time we met he called me Chloe."

"One of those, huh?" Noelle said with a shrug.

"He's a grown man who works with celebrities all the time. Don't you think he'd be over his fantasy crush?" Merry's anger returned. She wanted to smash something.

"Chloe was smart, she was easy to be with and she wasn't judgmental. You were the real star of that show, not Maddie. Every week, you saved Maddie's bacon and she got the guy while you stood back and let her. You were all the things a girlfriend, or a mom, is supposed to be, and you were as cute as a button. I understand why he's crushing on Chloe. You are Chloe. That character was never a stretch for you."

"Chloe was boring. Are you saying I'm boring?"

"Chloe was never boring. She was sweet, loyal, smart and she always had the right answer. If I'd been a guy, I might have had a crush on her, too."

"Sometime I wish I'd gotten the angry, bitter, jealous sister instead of you."

Noelle laughed. "Maybe I am and I'm just acting like I'm not."

"You're too understanding." Merry handed her sister another bear.

"It's a gift." Noelle placed the bear on another shelf and stood back to admire her display. She'd tossed little plastic snowflakes on the shelves and hung silver tinsel around the room. Lights had been twisted around the counter and doors. The store had a festive feel.

Outside, the sound of water rushing from a hose drew her to a window. Cleanup had started in earnest. Two maintenance men washed the walls of each store while a third scrubbed the concrete walkways. Hammering from the area around the roller coaster told her demolition had begun. She'd done a tour of her Christmas displays and only two had been scorched, though a third by the roller coaster had been completely lost. She wasn't going to worry about it.

"What was your intention with Daryl? Make Jake jealous?"

"No. I felt stupid because he wanted to sleep with Chloe, not me." Jake came around a corner and Merry watched him disappear down a path toward the carousel. The carousel had escaped damage, though it was covered in soot.

"He wasn't sleeping with Chloe. He knew who he was sleeping with." Noelle put an arm around Merry and hugged her. "I think you wanted a reason not to see him, not to continue with this affair, not to fall in love."

"Too late," Merry said sadly. "That's why I ran. I don't want to fall in love."

Noelle stepped back, surprise on her face. "That's a big reveal."

"Are you teasing me?"

"I'm not teasing you. Maybe a little." Noelle gave Merry another hug. "What's wrong with falling in love?"

"'Cause my life is not in order."

"What do you mean?"

"I'm not where I want to be."

"Where do you want to be?"

"I'm rootless. I guess I just thought I'd be further along in my career."

"You're only twenty-nine years old." Noelle gave Merry a little shake. "Lighten up. You're doing fine. My career is the one falling apart right now. The economy really ate into my business. I create art with glass. Who wants to buy artistic glass when they're worried about paying the mortgage? If business doesn't pick up for me soon, I'm going to have to move back in with Mom and Dad, and I definitely don't want to do that."

"You can move in with me. I have an empty bedroom. In fact, I have two," Merry said. "I didn't know business was bad. You just went to San Francisco to talk to a buyer."

"He's not buying. And moving in with my sister is just as bad as moving back to our parents' house."

"Not when your sister is this hip, cool chick, who isn't going to judge you or give you a curfew." Merry forgot Jake at her sister's revelation. How could Noelle not have told her? Merry told her everything.

"You're not going to distract me from talking about your life."

"Darn," Merry said with a small chuckle. "I gave it a try."

Noelle went back to placing her glass pieces on the shelves. "That's why I love you, big sis."

"The invitation is open, should you ever need to move. Now that we have your store in order, I have stuff to do."

Noelle jumped in front of the door. "No. No. No. If you love Jake, then go for it. He knows exactly who you are. Stop running away from him." She stepped aside.

Merry gave her sister a kiss on the cheek and left.

A man walked toward her, and for a moment she thought it was Jake.

"Mr. Chapman," she said in surprise.

Bernard Chapman was a short, round man in his early sixties with black hair going gray at the temples, which gave him a distinguished look.

"Merry, I was looking for you."

"Why?" she asked curiously.

"I took a long walk around this park and I'm pretty impressed with what you've accomplished."

For a run-down park, she thought. "Thank you, Mr. Chapman."

She showed him around while she assessed the damage from the fire.

"Very nice, Merry. Would you consider coming back to work for me, directing the set-design department?"

"At the park?"

"No, the studio."

She wanted to be unpleasant and ask if Lisa wasn't working out, but she didn't. Instead she smiled pleasantly even though her heart pounded. She had worked so hard for him and now he was offering her her dream, but she wasn't quite sure if that was what she wanted now. She had so many other opportunities. "I'd have to think about that, Mr. Chapman."

He smiled at her. "Please do."

"Will you give me until after Christmas?"

He thought for a second and then nodded. "Your new position would be with a substantial pay raise."

"I still need to think about it," Merry replied. She gazed around the park, aware of how much it, Jake and his father had come to mean to her.

"I'll be waiting." He held out his hand and she shook it. He walked away, still looking around.

She watched as he got into his Mercedes and drove away. Only then did she turn back to continue looking over the park.

Considering how close the fire had come, damage was minimal, though the smell of smoke was going to take time to dissipate. She found herself heading toward the carousel. She stopped behind a palm tree and watched Jake as he checked the carousel for damage. He carefully ran his hands over each horse, and Merry remembered how his hands had felt on her. He'd been so gentle, so sweet. Had she misread him?

"I need to apologize," Merry said as she stepped up to the carousel.

Jake paused. He loved the carousel, and she remembered their ride on it and how the music had sounded. She stepped up onto the platform. The horses were gritty with dust and smoke, but seemed undamaged.

"For what? You have nothing to apologize for. Maybe for ditching me for Daryl, but nothing else."

"That was not my best strategy." She still felt guilty using Daryl the way she had. But at least he'd learned they would never be a couple and Daryl had gone off on his happy way, already planning his next conquest.

"I agree. It wasn't," Jake said. "How about we talk over dinner tonight? My treat. The steak house at the Mission Inn?"

She found herself smiling. "Dinner it is." She walked away humming.

The steak house at the Mission Inn was elegant and comfortable. Jake drove, promising her he would take her back to the park to retrieve her car after their meal.

Merry twirled the stem of her wineglass while watching Jake. He looked completely at ease as he perused the menu. She would have preferred Andy's Crab Shack in Venice Beach, but that was a tough enough drive on a weekend. On a Monday it would be horrible.

"Are we going to make the opening?" he asked, after the waiter had taken their order.

"Everything will be fine." Merry buttered bread and took a bite. She almost closed her eyes in ecstasy. This was bread to die for. "The soot is coming off and only two displays need painting. I have volunteers coming out of the woodwork. Even your friend Bonnie showed up today to help clean. There are a lot of people in the community who love your father, and they want the park to reopen on time. You father gave me permission to give away free opening-day tickets. I think we're going to have a packed house." She smiled.

"I talked to The Brothers J today. They've agreed to play for free if we'll share the merchandise receipts. They've agreed to ninety percent of the net."

"Good. I designed a special T-shirt for them to commemorate the opening and their first appearance together in ten years." Just talking about opening day made her excited. The fire had been a setback, but the damage was fixable.

"They'll be excited about that."

"I took a photograph of them and combined it with Benny the Bear in Photoshop. We'll have hats, mugs and other merchandise to go along with it." She thought the graphic had turned out pretty well. John had loved it.

"I'm sure we'll sell a ton," Jake replied.

"Are you excited?"

He studied her for a second. "I didn't think I would be, but yeah, I am. My dad has worked really hard on this and maybe he is doing the right thing after all."

"And you're not worried about me stealing his money anymore?"

"You're going to get a lot of job offers from this. You'll be able to write your own ticket. What are you planning to do?"

She didn't tell him about Mr. Chapman's offer. She didn't want to share it until she'd figured out what her reply would be.

"Honestly, I have no idea." She'd talked to John earlier about cutting back on her time at the park, and he'd agreed she should explore other opportunities. Now that the designs were all set up, she wouldn't have to be at the park every day. She could work from home and accept some freelance jobs. She could afford to pick and choose what she wanted to do.

"I talked with your father today about my future. But I want you to know the park will always be my first priority." She'd come to love the park and John. And... Jake. Not seeing him every day and having to account for every penny would make her days less fun, but she'd survive. "Doing set design for music videos is quick, easy work that pretty much pays a crapload of money." The extra money would afford her some luxuries she didn't allow herself now.

Their dinner came and the conversation drifted off. Merry realized she was quite comfortable with Jake and relaxed even more knowing she didn't have to fill the time with conversation.

After their meal, Jake drove her back to get her car. The parking lot was empty except for her car. The night air was crisp and cool. A full moon hung heavy in the dark sky. Though the smell of smoke continued to linger, it was a lot less offensive than it had been earlier.

Jake opened her door and stepped out. He took her hand and said, "Come on."

"What?" she asked breathlessly.

He unlocked the gate in the chain-link fence and pulled her inside. He led her down the path toward the carousel.

"Stand here." He jumped on the bed of the carousel and walked through.

Merry waited, entranced. Like Jake, she loved the carousel and was happy it had escaped any damage. A second later, the carousel lit up. Someone had wrapped the horses, poles and benches in Christmas lights.

Merry clapped her hands. "It's beautiful."

"Come on," Jake called.

She jumped onto the carousel and in a second it started moving. The lights began to blink as the horses moved up and down on their poles. Christmas music blasted out.

Jake jumped on the carousel and came to stand next to her. "What do you think?"

What girl wouldn't get swept up in the romance of this? Especially with this man. " I love it."

"Trial run," he said.

He put an arm around Merry and pulled her close. She snuggled against him. He was warm and his breath fanned her cheek. She closed her eyes. He kissed her. His lips were soft against hers.

The magic of Christmas washed over her. Santa Claus had a large list to fill for her.

She slid her arms around his neck and let the kiss go on and on. The memory of their one night together made her body tingle and grow hot. The feel of his body against hers sent her into a passion so hot, she didn't think she'd ever feel normal again.

His kiss became more ardent, his lips covering hers, his body pressed tightly against her. Merry slid back against a bench while relaxing in his embrace. This was exactly where she wanted to be. He bent his head, his lips brushing her forehead, down the side of her face to her cheek and then to her mouth again. The lights, the music, the magic made her legs rubber, and she slid down to sit on the bench. Jake followed her down, one hand brushing her neck, the other tangled in her hair.

She wanted this ride to go on and on. She wanted the feeling to never end, to discover the never-ending story.

"About Saturday," Jake said when the kiss ended. "I wanted to explain…"

She held her hand up. "Do you smell something?"

He sniffed. "Yes, but I don't know what."

She took a moment to calm herself, closing her eyes and trying to identify the acrid smell of… "Gasoline."

Chapter 13

Jake took a deep sniff. Merry was right. "Gasoline."

He looked around, trying to figure out which direction it was coming from. The wind had stilled and the smell surrounded him.

"Should we call the police?"

"Let's investigate first." Jake turned in a circle. "It might be something that we can handle."

"I don't know, Jake. I have a bad feeling."

He powered down the carousel and turned off the lights. His eyes needed a moment to adjust to the darkness.

"This way." He grabbed her hand.

They ran around the rides and the miniature golf courses. The smell was growing stronger. Jake skidded to a halt at the first of the retail stores. He heard a small explosion. Flames rose.

He fumbled with his phone and almost lost it. Quickly

he dialed 911 and reported the fire. "Get a fire extinguisher."

Merry ran to a fire station and grabbed the extinguisher off the bracket. Jake grabbed another one. He ran toward the fire, the smell of gasoline so overpowering he started to cough.

He activated the extinguisher and pointed it at the flames. Something hit him in the back and he sprawled forward. He felt another strike on his back and when he turned, he found Harry Constantine reaching to twist the extinguisher out of his hands.

"Let it burn," Harry screamed at him. "Let it burn." He punched Jake in the face.

Jake heard a scream and in the next moment, Merry had jumped on Harry's back and was pummeling his head.

"Stop!" she screamed. "Stop."

Jake dropped the fire extinguisher and helped Merry subdue Harry. While he held Harry, he directed Merry to the fire. In the distance, he heard sirens. Help was almost here.

"Let it burn," Harry cried.

Jake grappled him. "Why, Constantine?"

Harry twisted to look at Jake. "You should've just sold me the damn property. My offer was more than fair. I had this deal completely sewn up and then your father... your father..."

"My father didn't want to sell." His father had made the right decision.

With his face highlighted by the flames, Jake could see anger tight on the other man's face.

Merry sprayed the flames. Jake would have helped her, but he needed to keep Harry subdued. The sirens had grown louder. Harry struggled harder.

"I'm ruined." Tears leaked from Harry's eyes. "I'm ruined."

Fire trucks poured into the parking lot, followed by several police units. Men poured out.

"I'm ruined," Harry sobbed.

"You're ruined no matter what now," Jake said. He let his grip relax now that the police had arrived.

Harry took advantage of the moment, twisting free and running. Jake took off after him. Harry turned and swung a fist, hitting Jake in the shoulder. Jake grunted. For an out-of-shape man, Harry packed a powerful punch. Jake jumped him and they both fell to the ground. In the next second, two police officers stood over them, their guns drawn. Jake got to his feet. The smoke from the fire made his eyes gritty. He saw the fire department taking charge and moving Merry away from the flames.

Detective Mars pulled handcuffs out of his pocket.

"I think this man is your arsonist." Jake stood aside as Mars pulled Harry to his feet.

"You may be right."

Merry ran up to Jake. "Are you all right?"

"I may have a bruise or two tomorrow, but I'm okay."

Merry grabbed him, her arms sliding around his neck. "I was so afraid he'd hurt you."

"He didn't," Jake reassured her. He put his arms around her and held her close, watching the flames slowly being subdued by the fire department. They all had fire extinguishers and soon the fire was under control.

"Do you have somewhere we can talk?" Detective Pederson asked.

"My office is over here." Jake led the detective toward his office while Detective Mars took charge of

Merry, leading her to her office. Jake couldn't help a small chuckle. Divide and conquer came to mind.

Merry talked to the detective, her arms swinging, her gaze meeting Jake's. She smiled. The detective gently moved her toward her office. She waved at Jake and he waved back. He marveled at her courage, but then again, he expected nothing less from her.

In his office, Jake called his father, then told Detective Pederson everything that had happened. By the time his father arrived, the detectives had released Jake and Merry. The fire department had everything under control. His father called Evelyn to let her know the arsonist had been captured, and then took Jake home while Merry went to a nearby motel.

The next morning, Merry bought new clothes at the mall and felt refreshed despite the lateness of her night. She arrived at John's office by midmorning, and when Detective Pederson arrived, she poured him a cup of coffee and sat down. Detective Pederson looked exhausted. She doubted he'd been to bed yet.

"To wrap things up," Pederson said, "we found a gas can with Mr. Constantine's fingerprints on it. We have evidence and a confession. He seemed to think that if he started a second fire, the insurance company wouldn't pay out and you'd be forced to sell."

"But why did he want this property so badly?" John asked.

"He told his investors that he'd already bought the property and they would be breaking ground for the next mall soon. He didn't expect your father to change his mind. And he couldn't go back to the investors with that information, so he thought he could force you to sell, Mr. Walters." Detective Pederson ran a hand over his face.

His clothes still smelled smoky and he needed a shave. "We also were able to tie him to the incendiary device. My partner found instructions on how to build one on Mr. Constantine's computer. We have enough evidence to convict him."

Merry frowned. "I sort of feel sorry for him."

"I don't," Jake said. He looked angry. "He caused a major fire that took millions of dollars to fight and tried to put my father out of business."

"Don't waste your pity, Miss Alcott," Detective Pederson said.

"I'm not saying what he did was right, nor am I condoning his behavior," Merry said. "He was just so desperate last night."

"I should have just stuck to my guns from the beginning," John said. "Then this wouldn't have happened."

"I'm sorry, too," Jake said. "I pushed for the sale and found the buyers. I should have just left well enough alone." He looked at his father. "I should have trusted you to know what's best for you."

John nodded. "Thank you. Now, we have a park to get ready. We're two weeks from opening and we have a lot of work left to do."

John walked the detective to his car. Jake refilled his coffee cup. Merry watched him.

"Fortunately, the building he set on fire hadn't been rented yet," Merry said.

"Can the building be saved? It was built in 1872."

"The contractor is looking at it now, but I think it's a total loss. The store next to it didn't catch fire, though it has a few scorch marks on the side. That's easily fixed. We're still on schedule."

"Good," Jake said. "You and I still have to work out our issues."

Merry grinned. "I know, but not today. I'm cool. Put the conversation on hold because I'm going to be putting in twelve- and fourteen-hour days for the next two weeks to keep everything on schedule."

"I can do that."

She nodded. "Okay. Let's get back to work."

On opening day, Merry was exhausted. For the past week, she'd rented a hotel room because she'd been too tired to travel back and forth from her home in Pasadena. But finally the day arrived and Merry found herself standing by the ticket booths watching guests make their way up the walkway to the entrance. For Black Friday, it was a great crowd.

She warmly greeted guests, recognizing a number of the volunteers who'd helped save the park from the fire. John stood inside the park, a walkie-talkie in one hand. He greeted the first customers even as he worked on last-minute issues. Jake had decided he would run the carousel for the day. Merry found that charming. He might not be attached to the park, but he loved the carousel.

The park itself was festive and bright, with Christmas lights hanging from every surface. The carolers stood just inside, singing as the customers came in. Christmas music blasted from the loudspeakers. Santa Claus would be arriving at noon in his own special parade. Various Christmas-themed activities were planned throughout the day all leading up to the concert, which would be ready to roll at seven o'clock.

"This is it," Noelle said.

"Are you ready?"

"This is going to be fantastic. The park is amazing. You did a great job."

"Thank you," Merry replied.

"What's next for you?"

"John isn't going to need me full-time now, so I'm contemplating a couple of video shoots."

"I'm impressed. Anybody interesting? I'd make a wonderful personal assistant."

Merry slanted a glance at her sister. "Maybe. Supposedly. One of them is in Cabo San Lucas."

"I'm already packed."

Merry laughed at her sister's enthusiasm.

"What about you and Mr. Hot Lips over there?" Noelle pointed at Jake.

"We'll have to see." Merry smiled at Jake and he smiled back. He was greeting people and handing out flyers for the concert. Fenya stood to one side, handing out info about her bakery and inviting people to come have a complimentary bite of her pirozhki. John hadn't succeeded in filling all the empty stores, but enough of them were open to satisfy people's needs to shop, and were offering Black Friday discounts.

"I'd better get going. My assistant doesn't come in till noon." Noelle walked off, her hips swaying. A couple of men turned to watch her and Merry suppressed a giggle.

"Today is going to be great," Jake said.

"What? Where is the real Jake Walters and what have you done with him? My goodness."

"Okay," Jake said. "I was wrong and I'm man enough to admit it."

"Where is your sister?"

He hitched his thumb over his shoulder. "She's beating down some five-year-old so she can be first on the Tilt-a-Whirl."

Now that was a real surprise. She was glad Evelyn made it to the opening. It would mean so much to John. "Really? I didn't see her come in."

"She came earlier with Dad. Just because we didn't want to take over the park didn't mean we didn't have good times here."

"Your sister made it sound like the end of civilization as we know it if your dad kept the park."

"She teaches physics. She needs a little drama in her life."

Merry shook her head. Eventually, she and Evelyn would be friends. Despite their differences, they had a lot in common.

"Jake," a woman said. Jake grinned at a tall, stately looking woman with shoulder-length blond hair, who was pushing two babies in a stroller with four more children following her. A tall, burly man followed the children as though herding them.

"Narissa, Cooper," Jake said in surprise. "I didn't expect you."

"We wouldn't miss this for the world."

Merry recognized Cooper James. Daryl Wicks admired him very much and often talked about him.

"Merry, this is Cooper James and his wife, Narissa, and their children."

What an assortment, Merry thought. The children ranged in age from what looked like six months to ten years. They looked to be of various ethnicities. Merry assumed they were adopted.

"Hello, Mr. Walters," the eldest one said, shaking Jake's hand politely. Solemnly, each child shook Jake's hand and said hello.

Merry was amazed at how well behaved all the children were and how neat and tidy they were. After a few minutes, the family walked into the park and Merry turned to Jake.

"Are they all adopted? The older ones look like him, but not like her."

Jake smiled. "That's a story for another day."

"This is one of your crazy client stories, isn't it?"

"Like I said, another day."

"You'd better get going, then. They look like they're heading straight for the carousel."

Jake took off after them, leaving Merry to continue greeting arrivals. Benny the Bear came to stand with her and children grouped around him, patting his fur. Parents urged their children closer for a photo op.

The trickle of customers tapered off. Merry decided to tour the park to make sure her displays were holding up. A child raised a scratched hand to her mother and Merry directed them to the first-aid station.

As the day wore on, the crowds grew denser. The lines for the rides grew longer. The food stalls were jammed and maintenance patrolled the picnic areas, cleaning up as each table emptied. John was adamant about keeping a clean park.

By dinnertime, the crowds had doubled as people arrived for the concert. Merry went backstage to watch The Brothers J get ready for their concert.

"This is the best day we've had in ten years, even with all the comp tickets you and I gave out," John said. He sat on a box, looking tired and a little bedraggled but happy.

"And it's going to get better."

"I stopped by the ticket office and people are buying yearly passes like nobody's business." John gave her a hug. "I don't know what's going to happen in the future, but we're set for the next year."

"Don't tell your son I said this, but we'll worry about next year, next year."

John put his hand out and she shook it. "Deal. What's your next project?"

"Mardi Gras," she replied. "I'll have the preliminary sketches for you next week. All the sets we have now can be easily repurposed with a little paint and imagination." Merry already had the designs in her mind. Now that the park didn't need her on a daily basis, she could get the next designs done quickly. After Mardi Gras would be Easter, then the Fourth of July, Halloween and back to Christmas again. She'd allowed for some minor variations to account for Valentine's Day, St. Patrick's Day and a few other one-day celebrations. Her mind churned with all the possibilities. It was one thing to get people here for a day but another to get them to come back.

"I know you'll do just as marvelous a job."

The Brothers J tuned their instruments. One waved at John and he nodded back.

Jake made his way to the staging area. Like his father, he looked tired. "Wow, what a day."

"It was epic," Merry said. She'd been on her feet all day.

"Where do we go from here?"

"We keep getting better."

He took her hand. "Where do you and I go from here?"

"I think I'm going to let you apologize to me very nicely. I didn't cheat your dad, and you have to admit that the park looks terrific."

"That's not the only thing I have to apologize to you for."

"And what would that be?"

He gave her a sidelong look.

"Do I need to give you two some privacy?" John asked, pushing himself to his feet.

"You don't want to see him groveling," Merry said with a grin.

"Am I going to grovel?" Jake asked.

"Son, if you know what's good for you, you'll grovel." John walked off leaving them alone.

"Merry," Jake said, "I had you wrong from the very beginning. I don't do that very often."

"That's because you see a celebrity and you automatically assume they're a train wreck."

"In my defense, by the time they get to me, they usually are."

Merry studied him. "I'm not a train wreck."

"I know that now. Figured it out all by my lonesome. I like you, Merry."

Her eyebrows rose. "I like you, too."

"You proved me wrong at every turn. I never thought I was making love with Chloe. I knew I was making love with you. I was trying to tell you that the reality of you was much better than the fantasy of Chloe. But my words came out wrong. I love you, Merry."

Her eyes went wide. "Really? You're absolutely positive you're not in love with Chloe?"

"Chloe was a nice girl. You're an amazing woman, and I want to spend my life with that woman, her mean cat and an amazingly detailed shoe collection."

Merry slid her arms around him. "I never thought I'd fall in love with a guy like you."

His eyebrows went up. "What's wrong with a guy like me?"

"Absolutely nothing." She kissed him, feeling light-headed at his declaration.

"Hey, you two," Noelle said. "Break it up. The concert is about to begin and we have some serious partying to do."

"We'll talk later," Jake said.

Merry chuckled. "I plan to do a whole lot more than talk." She linked arms with her sister and went out into the amphitheater just as the concert began.

Epilogue

Merry and Jake stood on the balcony waiting for the fireworks to begin. They'd taken a suite at the Mission Inn to celebrate New Year's and to take a little break from the park. When they'd left the park, it had been packed to the gills. She figured half of Riverside was there ready to celebrate New Year's.

"Mr. Chapman called me today," Merry said. "I didn't tell you, but he came by the park right after the fire and offered me a position running the set-design department. Apparently his niece didn't work out. She preferred to be a mime at the park."

Jake stiffened, his eyes questioning. "What are you going to do?"

Merry had so wanted that position, begged for that position, but her life had changed. "He called me this morning and I told him thanks but no thanks. I'm in the family business now." She held her hand out. The engagement ring sparkled as it caught the lights above them.

"Technically," he said, "it's going to be about six weeks before you're family."

"I would have been family yesterday, but you're the one who wants to get married on Valentine's Day."

"Your mother wanted the extra weeks to plan this."

"I'm okay with Valentine's Day, but I'm not so certain I like delaying our honeymoon until after tax season."

"Life with a person who deals with as much money as I do is all about keeping to a schedule."

A flare went off, lighting up the sky and bursting into white threads that spiraled up and out.

"The fireworks are starting," Merry said. She loved fireworks. She never missed a Fourth of July or New Year's Eve event that had them.

"Forget those fireworks. We're going to make our own." He pulled her into the suite, closed the doors behind him and led her to the bed.

* * * * *

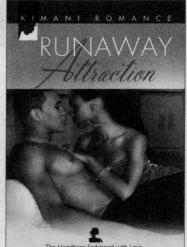

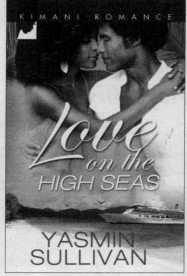

REQUEST YOUR FREE BOOKS!

2 FREE NOVELS PLUS 2 FREE GIFTS!

KIMANI™
ROMANCE

Love's ultimate destination!

KROM13F

A new novel of heated sensuality and dazzling drama, featuring her most unforgettable Madaris hero yet!

New York Times Bestselling Author

BRENDA JACKSON

A MADARIS BRIDE FOR CHRISTMAS

One by one, Madaris men have surrendered to their grandmother's matchmaking. But Lee Madaris isn't letting anyone else control his destiny. Which is why he needs to convince his hotel's gorgeous new chef, Carly Briggs, to agree to a marriage of convenience. Carly is tempted for many of her own reasons…but she's reluctant to complicate their working relationship. Yet soon, desire is clouding their no-strings arrangement.

"Brenda Jackson is the queen of newly discovered love, especially in her Madaris Family series."
—*BookPage* on *INSEPARABLE*

Available October 29 wherever books are sold!